Prologue

Gatling would have outdistanced the mounted militiamen if a bullet fired from far behind hadn't killed his horse. The animal screamed and dropped and Gatling went flying over its head and came down hard on his shoulder, and if there had been rocks instead of soft ground and thick prairie grass he would have been killed or badly injured. His shoulder felt as if it had been struck full force with an ax handle, but he didn't think anything was broken. He crawled behind the dead horse—there was no other cover—and loosened the leather thong behind the hammer of the long-barreled, single-action Colt .45. He checked the loads, eared back the hammer, and waited for them to come.

His Winchester .44-40 was pinned to the ground by hundreds of pounds of dead horse, with no way to get at it. The militiamen would be expecting fast, accurate rifle fire, so they'd be cagey at first. No surer way to get killed than to ride full tilt at a man in cover armed with a good repeating rifle he knew how to use. His ammunition belt sagged with rifle bullets, but that wouldn't do him any good. The rifle he couldn't get to was a fine weapon, with a smooth lever action and a rear sight, and the long barrel made it more accurate than the carbine.

There were eight militiamen, and they rode up and dismounted out of rifle range and took cover in a shallow dip in the prairie. Using his binoculars, he saw them crawl up to the rim of the hollow, their rifles pushed out ahead of them. They were armed with British Army Lee-Medford rifles, good enough for military hardware except the bolt action had a tendency to be stiff.

They opened fire, but the range was long; a few bullets sang over Gatling's head or plowed into dead horseflesh; the other bullets didn't even come close. Gatling, however, knew their shooting would improve when they got closer and took their time. He didn't shoot back because a revolver was useless at that range, and the moment they heard the sound of the Colt they would know he wasn't armed with a rifle. Six loads in the .45 were all the pistol bullets he had left. He had used up his .45 shells fighting his way out of the botched ambush and in the running fight that had followed. The militiamen's horses were farm animals, strong rather than fast, and he was ranging far ahead when the long shot killed his horse.

They kept up a heavy fire, but so far they hadn't tried to circle around and shoot at him from behind. Gatling thought that was sensible. The dip in the prairie was the only cover they had; for miles in every direction the grassland looked as flat as a floor. Gatling knew the eight men out there were afraid of his rifle, and he hoped they'd go on being afraid for as long as possible. But he knew they would attack sooner or later. They were sure to try something.

The firing stopped, and he glassed their position without seeing anything. Obviously they were deciding what to do. Gatling knew he had killed their sergeant during the poorly planned ambush—the man had had stripes on his dark green uniform—so there would be arguments.

TEST FIRE

Two men were out in front of the others and Gatling killed them with three shots. He pulled the "horseshoe" pistol from his belt and fired the round in the chamber. The .32-caliber bullet made a sharp, cracking sound in contrast to the boom-boom of the heavy military rifles. A man staggered and went down but got up again. Gatling fired fast and the odd pistol worked perfectly. It fired so fast he didn't know how much ammunition he was using up. The pistol was an autoloader with a short hammer action and he was literally spraying them with lead. Three of them were down with bullets in many parts of their bodies. There was no more yelling; they were too surprised to yell. Gatling was just as surprised as they were. . . .

The Gatling Series by Jack Slade:

#1: ZUNI GOLD
#2: OUTLAW EMPIRE

BORDER WAR

JACK SLADE

LEISURE BOOKS NEW YORK CITY

A LEISURE BOOK

July 1989

Published by

Dorchester Publishing Co., Inc.
276 Fifth Avenue
New York, NY 10001

Copyright©1989 by Dorchester Publishing Co., Inc.

All rights reserved. No part of this book may be reproduced or transmitted in any form or by any electronic or mechanical means, including photocopying, recording, or by any information storage and retrieval system, without the written permission of the Publisher, except where permitted by law.

The name "Leisure Books" and the stylized "LB" with design are trademarks of Dorchester Publishing Co., Inc.

Printed in the United States of America

Minutes dragged by and nothing happened. Flat behind the dead horse, Gatling knew the charge would be murder, not gun-running, if they took him alive. He had killed two militiamen fighting his way out of the ambush, so he would be tried by a military court and shot.

It was March and it was bitterly cold; the sky was blackened by rolling clould formations. Colonel Pritchett, head of the Maxim Company in New York, had sent him to Saskatchewan to deliver a large shipment of weapons to the *metis*, mixed-blood rebels led by Louis Riel, a former schoolteacher and current fanatic. The *metis*—hunters and trappers and farmers—had lived in Saskatchewan for many years and considered it their land, though they didn't legally own it. Their claim hadn't been challenged as long as the old Hudson's Bay Company had owned Saskatchewan and adjoining territory. Now the Canadian Government owned it, and shortly after it took possession, the surveyors, engineers, roadbuilders, and officeholders moved in. The Hudson's Bay Company had allowed the *metis* to live as free as the wind; the British Canadians had more "enlightened" ideas. Seeing their way of life threatened, the *metis* were now in open rebellion. . . .

The firing started again, and this time it was heavier than before. They were firing as fast as they could work the bolts of their rifles. Gatling raised the binoculars and saw two mounted men riding out of different ends of the hollow. Rifle fire became even heavier as the two men galloped forward, keeping away from the hail of lead the others laid down between them. Gatling kept his head down, but knew he'd have to shoot back or they'd ride over him,

They came recklessly, and maybe they thought he was unconscious or dead. The shooting stopped and they were riding at him from two sides, yelling as some men did when they were angry or afraid. Both men carried handguns because it was next to impossible to use a bolt-action rifle on the back of a galloping horse. They fired three or four shots and kept coming. The hoofs of their heavy mounts shook the ground and they were still yelling.

Gatling raised up and shot them out of the saddle. It took two bullets to kill the man on the left. As he fell his boot got tangled in the stirrup and he was dragged for about 50 yards until his body rolled away from the running horse. Three rounds were left in the Colt, and six militiamen.

Heavy fire came from their position. He had killed two men, but the sound of the handgun had given him away. Now they knew they didn't have to face rifle fire; if he had a rifle, he would have used it. Suddenly the firing stopped and through the binoculars he saw them crawling out of the hollow and into the grass. It was hard to see them in the tall, waving prairie grass. The men he killed had dropped their pistols, but it would take too long to find them, if he found them. He stayed where he was. Now and then he caught a glimpse of a dark shape in the grass; that was when a man was too big to effectively hide himself; the others he couldn't see at all. Nothing he could do but wait for them to get close enough to charge his position.

If he had been close to a belt of trees he would have made a run for it. But they would probably have brought him down with concentrated fire. The militia—farmers, blacksmiths, storekeepers, and the like—called up for emergency duty, were generally poor shots, but all it took was one bullet to kill or wound a man. And if they failed to kill him with rifle fire, they would mount up and ride him down, no matter how fast he ran. Still and all, if there had been thick timber to run to, he would have risked it.

He reached into the pocket of his lined canvas coat and took out the 40-shot .32-caliber pistol with the "horseshoe" magazine. That was what they called it, but it wasn't shaped like a horseshoe; the magazine was a perfect half circle of metal; one end of it fitted into a slot below the muzzle, the other was inserted into the pistol in front of the firing pin. Pressure from a spring pushed the rounds forward. The first round was released by thumbing back the hammer. After the first round was chambered, the shooter could fire as fast as he liked. For once, Gatling was about to use a weapon he hadn't test-fired.

Colonel Pritchett had given him the unusual weapon just before he'd taken a hansom cab to Grand Central Depot. "No time to see if it works," the colonel had said. "You have to be on the train with the guns. Take it along. The men who invented it, two brothers, swear it works, but I doubt if Mr. Maxim will buy the patent from them. These two brothers have produced a small number of 'horseshoe' pistols, as they call them. Midwestern drollery. They sent this one to me. Test it when you can, but don't let your life depend on it. . . ."

Gatling thumbed back the hammer and felt the first round click into the chamber. So far, so good. It might not work at all; inventors sent Pritchett weapons that could hardly be believed. But it was all he had to work with after he fired the last three rounds of .45 ammunition. The .32-caliber bullets in the "horseshoe" pistol weren't man-stoppers, but it would make a difference if he could get off 40 shots. The colonel said the spent shells were ejected up and forward.

It started to rain hard. The wind-driven downpour flattened the grass in seconds. Yelling like wildmen, the six militia troopers sprang to their feet and charged, firing their rifles as they ran. But bolt-action rifles were best used from a stationary position, and if they had knelt down and fired in the British manner, they would have had a better chance of killing him. Just the same, one bullet tore through the crown of his hat, another burned the side of the neck.

Two men were out in front of the others; he killed them with three shots. He pulled the "horseshoe" pistol from his belt and thumbed the first round into the chamber. The .32-caliber bullet made a sharp, cracking sound in contrast to the boom-boom of the heavy military rifles. A man staggered and went down but got up again. Gatling fired fast and the odd pistol worked perfectly. It fired so fast he didn't know how much ammunition he was using up. The pistol was an autoloader with a short hammer action and he was literally spraying them with lead. Three of them were down with bullets in many parts of their bodies. There was no more yelling; they were too surprised to yell. Gatling was just as surprised as they were.

He kept shooting until the firing pin clicked on empty. He didn't have a spare magazine, but there was no need for it. All six men lay still, dead or dying. The wind blew away the gunpowder smoke and fumes. The barrel of the "horseshoe" pistol was hot and he put it in his pocket after it cooled a bit. He would have to find .32-caliber ammunition for the weapon Colonel Pritchett didn't like and hadn't tested. It had saved his life.

He shot the wounded men in the head with their own rifles, then he collected the rifles and roped them together. Using a militia horse and a rope he rolled over the dead horse so he could get at his rifle. He pulled his saddle loose and put it on the militia horse. The dark sky was low and the rain hadn't let up. He looked at the dead men sprawled in the sodden grass. Sure as hell, this was a desolate place to die. There was nothing personal in the killing of these eight men. He had nothing against them, even though many militiamen were brutal Indian- and half-breed-haters who fought as much for loot as they did for their country.

He stripped the bandoliers from the bodies, tied the roped rifles to another horse, and headed back to the *metis*.

Chapter
ONE

Gatling was four blocks from the Maxim Company warehouse on Crosby Street when he heard the shooting. Gun battles were fairly common in the greasy, rubbish-strewn streets of the Lower East Side, where rival Jewish and Irish gangs, generaled by Monk Eastman and Shotgun Malloy, were forever warring over disputed territory. The police showed little interest in the constant bloodletting that went on between East Houston Street and Chinatown. Only the killing of somebody important, usually caught in a cross fire, could get them off their asses.

Gatling didn't give a damn who was shooting or who was getting shot. It was none of his business. An hour earlier he had eaten a thick steak and had drunk a quart-sized stein of good German beer in Luchow's Restaurant on Fourteenth Street. He didn't like New York, but it did have the best restaurants in the country. Apart from that, it was the asshole of Creation.

The shooting continued and it was still going on when he got to the corner of Crosby Street. It was coming from down by the Maxim Company warehouse, and that made it his business because he worked for Colonel Harry Pritchett, chief representative of the famous arms company in the United States. He drew the Colt .45 from its shoulder holster; there was no need to check the loads because he always checked his gun before he walked the dark streets of the Lower East Side. Down there, an experienced thug with a knife or a lead pipe could kill and rob as silently as an Apache.

The Maxim warehouse took up most of the block, and the only illumination in the street came from the flaring naphtha light above the thick steel door. It was so bright that it turned night into day, and it burned from sunset to daylight. The colonel was ever aware that his warehouse, with its three floors of the latest weapons, could become a target for Cuban rebels, Irish revolutionaries, or ambitious criminals.

There were no sidewalks. Packing cases, wooden skids and old nail barrels were piled high on both sides of the street. Gatling climbed up on a stack of skids while bullets kicked up sparks from the cobblestones. From where he was he could see two men in dark suits, their backs to him, trading shots with three uniformed guards from the warehouse. The shooters on both sides had knocked packing cases into the street and were using them as cover. Gatling wondered what the hell was going on. Two men would hardly try to take over a heavily guarded warehouse—or maybe they would. Before he climbed down he got a quick look at Colonel Pritchett, his cropped white head and black eyepatch, and heard the crash of his heavy Webley .455 revolver.

Gatling edged closer after he got down from the crate. One of the dark-suited men was reloading, the other was aiming careful shots. Gatling shot the second man in the back, shattering his spine; he collapsed like a rag doll. The first man had finished reloading and he snapped the breaktop Webley shut and tried to turn. Gatling shot him in the side of the head, then moved forward to pick up their revolvers. The man with the broken spine was still breathing, and he finished him off with a bullet through the forehead. Let the colonel go through their pockets; it was his warehouse, his street.

The colonel and the guards had stopped shooting, and away from the big light the street was dark and quiet. Gatling yelled his name. He yelled it a second time. "It's me, Gatling. Don't shoot. I'm coming out."

The colonel and the two guards came out to meet him. They had holstered their sidearms. "What the hell is going on?" Gatling asked. "Who were those men I killed?"

"British Secret Service agents," the colonel answered. "That man over there"—the colonel pointed—"they were trying to get at him before he got to me. They shot him once and were set to shoot again, but my guards ran out and opened fire. They didn't go far. No more talk. He may be badly wounded. We have to get him up to my office."

The colonel snapped his fingers and pointed. "Get rid of the bodies," he told the guards. A nod from the guards. They knew what to do.

Gatling and the colonel carried the wounded man into the warehouse and up the metal stairs that led to the office. He had been shot once in the back, probably with a dumdum or hollow-point bullet. The hole in his back was the size of a silver dollar and it was obvious that he was dying. Blood dripped all the way from the street to the leather couch opposite the colonel's desk.

The colonel turned him on his side so he could look at the wound. Gatling knew it was a waste of time. Nothing could be done for him.

"He's still alive," the colonel said.

"Not for long," Gatling said.

The bullet had penetrated a lung and was lodged there. Blood gouted from the dying man's mouth with every breath he took. Under the electric light, Gatling was able to get a better look at him. He was short and swarthy and had crow-black hair. A mixed blood. There was a lot of Indian in him.

"Colonel. . . ." Gatling started again.

"This poor beggar is why I sent for you," the colonel said. "A Canadian mixed-blood, one of Louis Riel's agents. He came here to buy guns. The *metis*, Riel's people, are preparing for a full-scale war against the Canadian Government." The colonel nodded toward the couch. "His name is Rideau, some sort of cousin of Riel's. Riel wrote me about him. He was to bring me a letter of credit and so on. I'll see if I can bring him round for a moment."

The colonel filled a small glass with brandy and poured a few drops into Rideau's gaping mouth. He coughed violently and opened his eyes. Already they had the glaze of death.

"In my pocket," he whispered, and then he died.

The colonel took the letter of credit from the dead man's pocket. With it was a letter and a list printed in capital letters. The colonel looked at the letter of credit before he read Riel's letter. That's the colonel, Gatling thought.

After going through the list, the colonel said, "Riel wants light and heavy machine guns. Maxims. Mauser rifles. Wonder where he heard about them. They're so new we just got our first shipment. You'll be testing the Mauser."

"Not on Canadians," Gatling said. "According to the papers, they're calling up the militia before they send in regulars. I'm not going to shoot a lot of farmers and storekeepers to test a new rifle. If Riel wants to take on the British Empire, that's his funeral. Soon as I deliver the guns and show them how to use them, I'll be heading back."

"Yes. Yes," the colonel said, getting back to the list. "He wants fifty Colt .45's and Webley .455's. Now listen to this. He wants five Hotchkiss Balloon Guns for shooting down observation balloons. The Balloon Gun is in the .70 caliber and fires an incendiary bullet that brings them down in flames. Last on the list: ten Hotchkiss 37-millimeter Revolving Cannons. A good list. Look it over."

The colonel handed Riel's letter and the weapons list to Gatling. The letter was brief and matter-of-fact. Riel said the bearer was Jean-Francois Rideau, one of his most trusted men. The letter of credit was to be presented at the Merchants Bank of New York, a private institution owned by a Mr. Garrett O'Brien.

"O'Brien is a Fenian," the colonel explained. "The Fenians want to drive the British out of Ireland. O'Brien started out as a boy teamster and now, thirty years later, he's a multimillionaire. He owns a huge department store on Sixth Avenue, among other things. He's been financing anti-British activities for years. He was the money behind the Fenian uprising in Ireland in 1867. A disaster, but it wasn't his fault. Now he sees a chance of getting back at Britain by backing Riel. O'Brien would back the Australian aborigines if he thought it meant trouble for Britain."

Gatling gave the list and letter back to the colonel, who took another look at the list before he put it in a drawer. "A routine shipment," he said. "Well, actually, not so routine. The Canadian and British authorities will be watching the border."

The dead man on the couch might not have been there.

"I'm thinking about that," Gatling said.

"Well, they can't watch every inch of it," the colonel said. "I've been looking at railroad maps, and Fortuna, North Dakota, might not be a bad place to cross. It's not actually on the border but eight miles below it. A branch line of the Northern and Fargo goes there. Big wheat country. The line does carry passengers, but its main business is hauling freight. However, it's your decision and your responsibility. We can't risk having the shipment seized. What do you think, my boy?"

Gatling was thinking of the long prison term he faced if the Canadians caught him with the guns.

"You know we'll be in violation of the Neutrality Act," he said.

"Correction," the colonel said. "You'll be in violation of the Neutrality Act. But have no fear. Certain senators and very influential businessmen have guaranteed that there will be no problems, legal or otherwise, on this side of the border. Not all of these men belong to the Annex Canada movement, but most of them do."

"Are those crackpots still around?"

"They most certainly are, and they would not be pleased to hear themselves described as crackpots. They are men of vision, something you couldn't possibly understand. Those who don't belong to the movement will be rushing to join. You know what they say about an idea whose time has come. These men believe the time is *now*. Mind you, these men had nothing to do with fomenting this rebellion, but as the conflict widens they believe the United States will have no choice but to enter—I nearly said *invade*—Canada to restore order. We can't have a civil war in our backyard, can we? If this seems high-handed, you must realize that there is no valid reason why Canada should exist as a separate country. It has a tiny population and is backward in many ways. But how it will flourish when it becomes part of the Union!"

"These politicians and businessmen want to steal Canada, is that it?" Gatling was getting tired of the colonel's speechifying. He knew the colonel had a long-standing grudge against Britain because he had been forced to resign from the British Army after many years' service. But his willingness to sell guns to his native country's enemies was something Gatling hadn't expected.

"Did you say *steal*?" the colonel said. "A poor way to put it, and a mistaken one. The men I referred to want the very best for Canada. They want Canada to realize its potential, something that isn't likely to happen under the present government or, to be candid, under any Canadian government. The dead hand of Great Britain lies heavy on that magnificent land—"

Somebody came to the door and knocked. It was one of the three guards who'd been in the shootout. He said, "Kelly and Mullins are taking care of what you said."

BORDER WAR   13

The colonel nodded. "Good," he said. "But spare me the details."

"I went through their pockets before they were taken away," the guard said. "They had money and good watches and keys, but no identification papers of any kind. Nothing to say who they was. No labels in their clothes neither. Their shoes, no maker's mark."

The colonel smiled after the guard left. "Those Secret Service bastards! They did for poor Rideau over there, shot the poor fella in the back. Heartless swine. They must have followed him from Saskatchewan, or they learned he was coming here and were waiting at the railroad station. Don't ask me how they got on to him. My guess is they planted a man in Riel's camp. One thing the bastards are is cunning. Watch out for them, Gatling, or they'll put a bullet or a knife in your back first chance they get."

"Thanks for the warning," Gatling said dryly. "Anything else you want to tell me?"

The colonel took his foul-smelling pipe from the desk drawer and proceeded to fill it with shag tobacco. That took a while. "Well yes, there is," he said. "For various reasons the Maxim Company must not be connected in any way with this enterprise. If the facts were revealed, it could be very awkward for Mr. Maxim."

The colonel struck a wooden match and the room began to fill up with blue-gray smoke. It smelled as if he had put horsehair in the pipe instead of tobacco.

"It would be awkward and embarrassing," the colonel said.

"Meaning the British might close his factories and kick him out of the country?"

"Crudely put but essentially correct."

"Then why do it at all?"

"Business. Mr. Maxim is first and last a businessman. He invents, manufactures, and sells weapons. He fills a need. What people do with his guns, after they buy them, is no concern of his. Wars were here thousands of years before Mr. Maxim was born, and they'll still be here thousands of years after he's gone. But we're straying from the point."

"Which is?" Gatling said.

The colonel said, "The guns that go to the *metis* will originate with the Superior Arms Company of Chicago. It's quite simple. They buy the guns here, from this very warehouse, then sell them at their own price."

Gatling knew every weapons dealer in the country. "There's no such company, Colonel."

"There is now," the colonel said. "And you are its sole owner. My lawyer went out there last week to set it up. He drew up the papers of incorporation, so it's all legal and aboveboard. There is even an office, small but quite all right for present purposes."

Gatling didn't like any of this. "Where's the office? Behind the stockyards?"

"Certainly not," the colonel said. "It's on Division Street. An arms dealer doesn't have to put on the dog. His weapons speak for themselves. Don't fret about the bloody office. You won't have to go there. It's enough that you exist, the office exists, and the Superior Arms Company is legally incorporated. Why the sour face, Gatling?"

"Do I get a salary as president of this cardboard company?" Gatling enjoyed trying to put the bite on the colonel for additional money. It never got him anywhere, but it got the colonel mad.

The colonel said irritably, "You'll get your usual fifty thousand, and that's all. Good Lord, man, where else could you make that much money? I know you give most of it to your benighted Zunis, but that's not my concern."

What the colonel said was true. He gave nearly everything he made to the Zunis, the peaceful farmers and herdsmen who had taken him in and raised him after his parents were murdered and scalped by Apaches. He had returned to the Zuni pueblo in New Mexico after many years in the white world to wage a one-man war against other Apaches hired by ruthless mining operators who wanted to grab the Zunis' copper-rich land. The colonel had come from New York to see how Gatling was doing with the Maxim Company weapons, and ended up fighting by his side. Before the war was won, the colonel had lost an eye.

The wall telephone shrilled and the colonel got up to answer it. "Be with you in a minute," he said, but whoever was calling kept him on the line for much longer than that.

"All our weapons are in perfect condition," the colonel told the caller.

Weapons! Gatling thought. Since he had come to work for the Maxim Company, his whole life had been weapons. It was a strange life, but he enjoyed it most of the time. He tested the latest weapons manufactured or distributed by Maxim. He tested them in combat, and got fifty thousand dollars for each assignment. He couldn't say how many men he had killed, but he never killed anyone who didn't deserve it. At the end of an assignment he had to write up a detailed report on how well the weapons worked, or didn't work. If there were flaws in their performance, that too went into his report. So far he hadn't tested a single dud.

"Bloody gas bag, that man," the colonel complained, hanging up the telephone. "But he's ready to buy one hundred thousand dollars' worth of guns, and that's the main thing. Where were we?"

"We were talking about the Superior Arms Company," Gatling said.

The colonel snapped his fingers, a habit he had. "That's all settled. Forget it."

"What about Riel, Colonel? Nothing I've read about him in the papers gives a clear picture of the man."

Lying back in his chair, the colonel blew smoke at the stamped-tin ceiling. "Riel is a bit of a mystery," he began. "He's a dreamer, but can be a practical man when he has to be. If you know his background, there's no point to repeating it."

"I know most of it," Gatling said. "There was an earlier rebellion?"

The colonel nodded. "At the end of '69. It lasted into '70. But it was the Red River region, east of Saskatchewan. The circumstances were much the same. The *metis* had lived there for generations, keeping themselves aloof from the rest of Canada. A sort of separate country, you might say. Then the Canadian Government moved in, the *metis* rose up, but were finally defeated by a well-armed force of seventeen hundred men. Riel escaped to Montana, where he became a schoolteacher, an American citizen thirteen years later. The British Canadians insist he's insane."

"Is he?"

The colonel lurched forward in his chair, another of his habits. He lay back when he was at ease, lurched forward when he was agitated. "I don't know if he is or not. He did spend some time in *two* asylums in Montana. But a lot of dreamers are high-strung and do strange things. I'm inclined to believe he was locked up because of what would seem to be his crazy ideas. I never met the man, but the Pinkerton Detective Agency has a thick file on him. Alan Pinkerton himself doesn't think he's crazy, and I have the greatest respect for Mr. Pinkerton's opinion. 'Dangerous and eccentric but definitely not insane,' is how Mr. Pinkerton phrased it."

The guard who had reported earlier came back to inform the colonel that Kelly and Mullins had returned.

"Good show," the colonel said. "Now listen to me, Eberhart. No one is to enter this building for the rest of the night. The door is to remain locked and bolted. If men come and bang on the door and say they're policemen, ignore them. I don't care how many badges they display, you are not to open that door. After Mr. Gatling and I leave, don't open the door until I return in the morning. Got it?"

The guard touched the peak of his cap in a sort of salute.

"Got it, sir."

"Good man, Eberhart," the colonel said, lying back in his high-backed chair. He glanced at Gatling. "Somehow I sense there is one question you haven't asked me. What is it? Out with it, man!"

"Well it's getting late, Colonel. I'll see you in the morning."

Gatling stood up. The colonel told him to sit down. Gatling remained standing.

The colonel lurched forward. "You're wondering why I'm selling guns that will be used to kill British soldiers. Let me tell you, sir, that I don't owe a goddamned thing to Great Britain or its pudding-faced queen." The colonel's tone was dry and bitter. "Will you please sit down, for Christ's sake?"

Gatling sat down. Why not hear the old bastard out?

"Sons of bitches kicked me out of the Army after thirty years of loyal service simply because I ordered my men to open fire on a bunch of dirty Afghan ragheads pretending to come in to surrender. We were outnumbered ten to one, but of course we had machine guns." The colonel showed his tobacco-stained teeth in a mean smile. "We had heavy Maxims and were ready for them. Oldest dodge in the world, that surrendering business. Get in close under the white flag, then out with the hidden weapons—and slaughter!"

Gatling knew Colonel Pritchett wasn't telling the truth. He had given the order to machine-gun 200 Afghans because Afghans had tortured and killed his only son, a 19-year-old second lieutenant. It had happened years before, enough time for the colonel to reshape the truth, to believe what he wanted to believe.

Usually the colonel was gray-faced; now his face was red with anger. "The Liberals in Commons made such a stink over a mob of filthy, murdering savages. You'd think I'd turned my guns on a bank-holiday crowd in Blackpool. I was forced to resign or face a court-martial. No pension—nothing. That's why I'm delighted to be able to send guns to Riel.

A fine Irishman, that fella."

Gatling stared at the colonel. "Riel is *Irish*?"

"Well, anyway, he's quarter Irish," the colonel said defiantly. "Quarter Irish, quarter Cree Indian, half French. But I'll bet on his Irish blood any day of the week. The Irish know how to break the British Lion's balls."

The colonel realized he was talking too much, giving away too much, and he tried to cover his embarrassment by switching the subject to the guns Gatling was to deliver to the *metis*. "I know it's getting late, but there is one thing we must get settled. I really can't see how we can pay you fifty thousand dollars if you don't test our weapons, especially the new Mauser rifle. A rifle that uses smokeless-powder ammunition is going to be very important, not just now but for years to come. Mr. Maxim thinks it will sell like hotcakes."

The hell with what Maxim thinks, Gatling decided. "I told you I won't kill farmers and storekeepers just to test a fucking German rifle. How much will I get if I just deliver the guns?"

"No more than ten thousand," the colonel said. His anger had disappeared. "However, we'll leave that open until you return. You may find yourself in a dangerous situation where you will have to kill to save your own life."

Gatling knew what the colonel was thinking, but it didn't make him angry. "Not if I can help it," he said.

"Well you never know," the colonel said in a silky voice. "As they say, circumstances alter cases. Good night, Gatling. I'll see you in the morning. Now I must check Riel's list against inventory."

Gatling stood up. "What about him?" he asked, meaning the dead man Rideau.

"Don't worry about it," the colonel said.

Chapter TWO

Gatling had to change trains in Chicago. There was another change at Bismarck, North Dakota, and now he was on the branch line of the Northern & Fargo, heading for the tiny farm town of Fortuna, eight miles below the Canadian border. Four wagonloads of crated weapons were in a freight car; the *metis* were to meet him at the depot in Fortuna. He hoped they'd be waiting when the train pulled in. A stranger in a dismal little station, with a huge stack of crates, would be regarded with suspicion. The local lawman might try to be helpful.

A freight train with one car for passengers, it made no great speed, although the prairie was flat all the way to the horizon and beyond. The passenger car was old and the cold wind blew through it from one end to the other. A pot-bellied stove raised the temperature by a few degrees; it kept them from freezing, and that's all that could be said for it.

Gatling was one of four passengers; the others were a gaunt farm woman, a drummer with a sample case, and a man who looked like a storekeeper. Neither of the men looked like a British Secret Service agent. The drummer was fat and elderly, the storekeeper wore thick-lensed spectacles that had been repaired with thin copper wire. But nothing was for sure. The British Secret Service, the best in the world, probably had people who weren't regular agents but acted as the eyes and ears of the worldwide spy organization. He had seen the farm woman on the train from Chicago; she looked very sick and might have been to see a medical specialist. The two men had gotten on at Bismarck.

The two British agents he'd killed in New York had been after Ridieu's papers. The loss of the letter of credit would hold up the gun deal for weeks, maybe months. Riel's letter and weapons list would be proof of the Maxim Company's involvement in the *metis* rebellion, and it would provide exact information about the kind of weapons Riel was buying. But for now the agents were probably at the bottom of the East River or far out in the harbor, dumped from the Staten Island ferry. No way they could report to their superiors that Rideau was dead. They would shoot no more people in the back with dumdum bullets.

Gatling looked out at the flat, featureless, snow-covered prairie. Here the country was frozen solid in winter, oven-hot in summer. The few houses he saw were miles apart, and always close to the house was the creosote-blackened barn, the silo, the windmill.

The disappearance of the two agents would cause a great flurry of activity. Senior pipe-smokers would meet in offices in New York and Toronto and Montreal to discuss the situation. Cables would be sent to London.

Colonel Pritchett suspected there was a British agent among Riel's guerrilla fighters. The colonel was a wise old bird, and he was probably right. "A swarthy French-Canadian or a real mixed-blood who hasn't been with Riel very long, that's what you have to look for," the colonel had said. "Or, come to think of it, a British Canadian who knows the Saskatchewan country and speaks the *metis* dialect. He doesn't have to be all that dark-skinned. Some of the *metis* are as white and as fair-haired as Jenny Lind. Better keep a sharp lookout, my lad, because you'll be his prime target. You may deliver the guns, but if you're killed shortly thereafter, the *metis* won't know how to use anything but the pistols and the rifles. So far the rebellion hasn't gone beyond a lot of skirmishing and bushwhacking. Riel hasn't made a major move because he's still waiting for *metis* to arrive from the Far North. When they're all assembled, he will have an army of several thousand men, and if the Cree Indians get into the fight, he'll have a lot more than that.''

The train chugged along at 25 miles an hour. Holding a bible with a soft leatherette cover, the gaunt woman took a pill without looking at it, and without water. Slouched in his seat, the fat salesman nipped at a flat, brown pint bottle of whiskey. The storekeeper, who rode with his back to the engine, twitched his lips in disapproval. Cigar stubs littered the floor and the windows were dirty. The car hadn't been cleaned for a very long time.

The conductor-freight master came in to collect their tickets, and Gatling asked him how long to Fortuna.

'' 'Bout fifteen minutes,'' the man answered. ''Looks like more snow, don't it?''

Colonel Pritchett had said the main purpose of the British Secret Service was to delay the war as long as possible. The *metis* had guns but most of them were old and often repaired. A lot of them were muzzle-loaders, cap-and-ball rifles; some of the dirt-poor *metis* were armed with flintlocks; only a handful of their weapons were new.

Without up-to-date weapons, the colonel had said, Riel didn't stand a chance. The four wagonloads from the Maxim Company would make a difference—that is, if Gatling managed to deliver them. From the strained look on the colonel's face, Gatling knew the colonel wasn't sure the shipment of weapons wouldn't be seized the moment it was across the border. Gatling wasn't sure himself. His only advantage was that the two agents were dead and their superiors had no knowledge of when the guns would be delivered, or where.

The colonel hadn't told Gatling to cross the border at Fortuna. Pritchett had favored Fortuna because it might be the place they would least suspect. But in the end it was Gatling's decision. If he got caught or killed, it would be his own doing.

The shipment itself had been handled in a routine manner; it went out with all the other crated weapons that left the warehouse six days a week. Among them were 20 crates filled with junk and consigned to an address in Great Falls, Montana.

"Anything to confuse the bastards," the colonel said.

The conductor came back into the car and yelled, "Fortuna! Fortuna! We're coming into Fortuna, folks."

A light snow was falling and it was getting dark. The train moved slowly down the middle of the main street and stopped at the tin-roofed depot. Gatling swung down and looked for men and wagons. Nothing that he could see, unless the *metis* were keeping out of the way until the guns were unloaded and the train moved on. It was cold enough to kill anyone who stayed out in it too long, or didn't have the right clothes.

Gatling had his tally sheet ready when the freight crew began to unload the crates. They worked fast because of the cold, and some of the crates got some rough treatment, but the crates were well-padded, and Gatling didn't say anything. He just wanted the guns off the train and the train gone.

Dry snow was already dusting the crates when the train pulled out, its bell clanging to warn people out of the way. But there was nobody in the street, and few lights showed in the stunted houses on both sides of it. The man who came out of the depot office to watch the unloading had gone back inside. There were no freight charges to be paid. He checked that against a list he had, and went back to his stove.

Gatling had been waiting for 20 minutes in the bitter cold, his boots sticking to the frozen mud of the street, when a man wearing an ankle-length buffalo coat and a fur hat with earflaps came down the street. A badge with a felt backing was pinned to the front of his coat. His breath steamed in the cold air.

"Cold enough for you?" he said to Gatling. "All this freight belong to you? There's a right power of it."

Gatling said it did, but gave no further explanation. Dakota people were known for minding their own business, and maybe this furry lawman would mind his. For the moment, he did. After bullshitting about the weather for a minute or two, he said good night and continued with his rounds. But Gatling knew he'd be back if Gatling waited too long. His ingrained policeman's suspicions would get the better of his reticence, and then there would be questions. It might not come to anything, he did own the stack crates and had papers to prove it, but where was he taking all this freight? The policeman would want to know. Everybody in Fortuna had to know about the trouble just across the border, so the policeman would ask questions he wouldn't otherwise have asked.

Gatling was clapping his gloved hands and stamping his feet when he finally heard wagon wheels crunching in the frozen snow. Four covered wagons with high sides emerged from the slanting screen of snow and came to a halt where the crates were stacked. A big man jumped down from the first wagon; the driver stayed where he was, holding the horses steady.

"Dese are de guns?" the big man asked. He was inches taller than Gatling, who was six-two, and a lot heavier. So heavy that his gut hung over his broad belt. It was cold as hell, but he had his sheepskin coat open. His hair was long and black, his stubbly beard dirty white. Missing front teeth gave him a sinister appearance.

Gatling nodded in answer to his question. "Why are you

so late?"

"Militia try to stop us, ask us question. We have to kill dem. Den we have to chop hole in ice and put dere bodies in lake. We put chains on dem so dey don't come up when dere bellies are big with gas. We have to do all dat 'cause not so good if other militia find bodies. Dey find bodies dey tink—dey know—de *metis* have come far south."

"Better start loading," Gatling said. "Before the town policeman comes back this way."

"He come back we kill him," the big man said.

"No killing," Gatling said. "Will you start loading the guns?"

The big man gave a low-pitched whistle and his men got down from the wagons and started loading. Knowing what was in the crates, they handled them with great care. The snow, heavier now, was beginning to stick, and Gatling wondered if they'd make it across the border without getting stuck.

Watching the men, the big man said, "I am Gabriel Dumont." He turned to Gatling and held out his hand.

"I'm Gatling." They shook hands. Gatling said, "This godamned weather—"

"No," Dumont said. "We don't damn dis weather, de snow, we bless it. It hide wagons, it hide us, it hide de guns. Wagons make not so much noise in snow. We have grease de wheels, tie everything down dat rattle. We don't talk when we get close to border. No militia by border when we cross, but if dey have come dere, we creep pass dem like ghost."

The seven *metis* loaders finished loading the first wagon and started loading the one behind it. Gatling looked down the snowy street. No sign of the policeman.

"Can you get the wagons through in deep snow?" Gatling asked.

The big man showed his gapped teeth in a smile. "We get trough, you bet. We have put spikes on wagon-wheels and dey grip de ice under de snow." He looked up at the sky, raised his head, and sniffed. "Not so much snow. It stop soon. We get across. Now I help my men."

Dumont and Gatling pitched in, and the loading went faster. The *metis*, silent dark men, stared at Gatling, who wondered if they took him for an Indian or a mixed-blood. People often did because of his deeply tanned skin—the result of a childhood spent under the blazing New Mexico sun, at the Zuni pueblo—and his Indian-black hair. A lot of white men had dark looks, especially in the South—he'd been born in Mississippi—but it was more than that. It was the way he carried himself that marked him for an Indian or a half-breed. But if people wanted to take him for an Indian, that was fine with him.

They finished loading the last wagon and moved out, and as they did the station man and the policeman came out and watched from under the overhang of the roof. The policeman had come back and gone into the depot by the back door. He had been watching them all the time. Gatling wondered what he would do. Maybe nothing. He could be in the pay of the British Canadians, getting money to report on the movements of strangers, and a telegraph message to Canada could be relayed through Bismarck and Chicago. No line went north from Fortuna.

When they were clear of the town, skirting the railroad line until the road turned north, Gatling said to Dumont, "I'm going to cut the telegraph line. You got a hatchet?"

Dumont smiled his Halloween pumpkin smile. "Sure we got hatchet. We got everything 'cept sewing machine."

Dumont was driving and he halted the wagon, spoke in French to the man riding in back with the guns, and got the hatchet. There was ice on the climbing rungs of the telegraph pole and the pole itself. Gatling climbed up into swirling snow, held on as best he could with one hand, and chopped through the wire where it came out of the porcelain insulator. The wire dropped to the ground. It could be easily repaired, but nobody was going to do it on this kind of night.

"Pret' good," Dumont said when Gatling climbed up on

the seat.

Half a mile from there, the wagons turned north. It was a better road than was usually found in remote farm country; most of the people here were Germans and Scandinavians, and they built their roads with the same care they gave to their silos and barns. The snow was deep, and underneath it was frozen mud and ice, but the powerfully built horses had studded shoes and the wagons moved along at a slow but steady pace. Dumont said they would reach the border in about three hours.

"Good horses," he said. "But de wagon dey are heavy and de horses have to rest. But we get dere. I am tinking how Louis's eyes will shine when he see de guns. He will not smile but his eyes will say he is pleased. Louis never smile and he does not laugh. I smile and laugh all de time. I laugh like jackass when I drink plenty whiskey."

Dumont reached under the seat and found a quart of whiskey. He uncorked it and offered Gatling a drink. Gatling said no thanks. Once in a while he went on a three-day drunk when he felt the need of it. He could be dangerous then, if anybody crossed him, so maybe there was an Indian somewhere in the family. He knew there wasn't; it amused him to think so. Beer was his drink, especially the good brown Pearl beer they brewed in Texas.

Dumont took two big swallows and put the bottle under the seat. He sighed with satisfaction. "Pret' damn good," he said.

"Don't laugh too loud," Gatling said.

Dumont laughed quietly. "You are funny man, Gatling. "I don't laugh big laugh till I drink full quart. When I drink two quart, dey hear me in Quebec. Ottawa fine French city, den de fuckeen British take it over, make it dere capital city. Capital city of all Canada. The *metis* live tousand of mile away from dere, why they bodder us?"

"The government is always bothering somebody," Gatling said. "How is the war going?"

"Real war not start yet," Dumont said. "We drive Mounties from dere posts in our country. We kill some redcoats. Rest of dem not come back. Militia come, not so many, and drive dem out like Mounties. Kill some. We put tail between dere leg, you bet."

The wagons rumbled quietly over the frozen road. For the first few miles the snow was thick and blinding; now it was easing off a bit.

"It still snow when we cross de border," Dumont said confidently. "De militia be dere, we fool dem. I hate de goddamn militia, dirty, rotten bastard son of bitch."

"Are they any good?" Gatling asked. "I mean, can they fight?"

"Sometime dey do, sometime dey run away. A lot of dem togedder, dey fight pret good. Scotchman and Englishman, not so much Irishman. De Scotchman hate de Irishman if he is Catlick. Irishman hate him back. No French Canadian in militia, dis part of de country."

"You think you can win?"

"We can beat de militia seven day a week. But I am smart man and know we cannot beat regular army Canadian and British soldier if dey send whole reg'ments, tousand of men. It is a guess what gov'ment will do. Louis tink dey will threaten us very strong, but when we don't bend dey will back off from real big war. But if dis war come, we will fight to de end."

Gatling had nothing to say to that. He knew the British Canadians wouldn't back off, not even if Riel armed every *metis* in Saskatchewan and the Northern Territories with modern rifles. They wouldn't back off because of national pride and, even more important, because Saskatchewan was rich in minerals and its soil as fertile as the American Midwest. Patriotism and greed, an unbeatable combination. After the *metis* were crushed they would be given some land, but it wouldn't be good land, and in the end they would be pushed out altogether.

"We must be getting close," Gatling said. They had been on the road for well over two hours; the horses had been rested twice. It was snowing lightly.

Dumont didn't say anything for a while; the big *metis* was brooding over something. "De militia, some of dem, have rape our women." His loud voice became low and snarling, full of hate. "Dirty *metis* women, de militia tink what does it matter. Dirty hoors, *metis* women, dey like to have white cock shoved in dem. I catch four militia dat rape *metis* woman and cut off dere balls."

Gatling just grunted. Sure as hell Gabriel Dumont would hang if the militia ever captured him.

"Bastard militia tink we have gold," Dumont went on. "Dey tink we get it in Northern Territory. What gold? We don't look for gold. We find gold de whole of Canada will be digging up Saskatchewan, one end to the udder. Gatling, we are hunters and farmers and we take fish in de river. Dat is all we want to do."

"Sure," Gatling said.

Dumont took a short drink of whiskey and wiped his mouth. "We talk quiet now. De border is dere, half a mile, no fence, no noting. Sometimes the militia cross de border couple of mile. No tonight. I go ahead now, see if we can cross without we have to fight. Keep horses steady, Gatling."

Dumont climbed down and disappeared into the darkness. The horses were strong, docile animals, but even if they hadn't been well-behaved, the weight of the wagon was enough to discourage any skittishness. The only sound was the horses' breathing; nothing moved anywhere in the great expanse of snow-covered prairie.

Dumont came back and climbed up beside Gatling. "Only two militia, I kill dem with my knife." Pleased with what he had done, he showed Gatling a huge double-edged knife. "They are in tent so not to freeze. But I know dey are half-freeze and stiff. I make little noise and one militia come out to see what is dere. I cut his throat, him not make a sound. Den the udder militia come out and I do de same for him. Now we cross and not have to shoot."

The wagons moved on. "Now we are across," Dumont said. "We are in Canada."

Canada means a lot to him, Gatling thought. Or at least this part of Canada. It was too bad the *metis* couldn't have their republic, or whatever it was they wanted. Canada was such a vast country, most of it empty. But whatever happened or didn't happen, it would be one hell of a mistake to get involved.

Dumont saw Gatling looking at his watch. "You better get back dere and sleep. Me, I sleep plenty on de way to Fortuna so I am not sleepy on de way back with de guns. Only time I am awake is when one of my men who go ahead come back and say militia hiding in trees by road. We leave wagons, creep up and kill dem, sink dem in lake. Den I go back to sleep. Go to sleep, Gatling. Dere is a long way to go."

"How long?"

"Maybe a week. We have to hide de wagons and sleep by day. Night and the darkness, dey hide us. De militia, dey patrol de roads in de daytime, de big roads. We travel on no big roads, keep away from de towns. Back roads not patrolled so much. We trust in God and so far he have listen to us. You think God is a Catlick?"

"The Catholics like to think so." Gatling knew the droll *metis* might be trying to pull his leg. The man was as dangerous as a man can get, but he was absolutely fearless, completely loyal to the cause he believed in. Behind all his talk there was a shrewd intelligence. A bad man to cross, he would be a good friend or an implacable enemy. Gatling liked him.

"I think I will sleep," Gatling said.

"Smart fella," Dumont said, then spoke to the man in back in rapid French. When Gatling climbed into the back of the wagon there was a blanket spread out on the floor, other blankets to cover him.

"Good night, my friend," Dumont called back to him after he lay down. "We will eat in de morning."

Chapter THREE

At 7:30 the next morning it was still dark except for streaks of gray light in the eastern sky. Snow was still falling. Breakfast was venison stew and strong black tea reheated over a tiny charcoal fire that glowed red, but gave off no smoke.

They were in a wide, flat ravine with high sides, about 900 yards off the road. Between the ravine and the road were trees; they had to edge around the trees to get in there without damaging the wagons. Snow already covered the tracks made by the wagon wheels. After they ate two guards would be posted in two shifts while the rest of them slept through the short daylight hours. It would be dark before five.

During the night when they halted to rest, grain, and water the horses, Gatling pried open the crate where the modified Light Maxim was packed. He had used it against the Apaches in New Mexico. The original gun had been made with a tripod; a metal seat was attached to the back support. The gun was very light—a man could hold it out at arm's length—and it was fired without a water jacket. The barrel was thick enough so the gun could fire 300 rounds without overheating. No water jacket, no spilling. The colonel's gunsmiths, working to Gatling's specifications, had fitted a short bipod to the end of the barrel, to replace the tripod and the seat. A steel and hard rubber grip was attached to the underside of the barrel, forward of the cartridge feed. The gun had a pistol grip and a trigger; the first shot put the gun on full automatic fire. To the right of the cartridge feed was a light metal box that held the 300-round canvas belt. This had not been changed. When the bipod was extended the shooter could lie behind the gun without showing too much of himself. Best of all, the shooter could pick up the gun and move in firing from the hip.

"What you do?" Dumont asked when he saw the machine gun. "We don't want militia to know we have machine gun and bolt rifle before de war start. If militia attack us, we will fight dem with rifle we have."

Gatling said, "If there's enough of them, we may never get to deliver the guns." He still didn't want to get mixed up in this war, but he wasn't going to stand there and let the militiamen kill him. Dumont had killed a few militiamen on the way south from Batoche, and he had killed two more at the border, which had been easy enough for a man of his cunning and ferocity, but what if they had to fight a militia patrol of 20 or 30 men armed with bolt-action rifles?

He told Dumont what he was thinking and Dumont said, "No patrol dat big. I know how de militia do things."

"All right," Gatling said. "Suppose it's not a patrol but a large force sent out to get us. Some farmer going home late could have seen us."

"Nobody saw us coming down from Batoche."

"You make better time coming down from Batoche. The wagons were empty and moved faster. Now the wagons are loaded down and we're moving like snails. Look, we have the best guns in the world in these wagons. We won't use them if we don't have to. But if we do use them, we have to make sure nobody runs away to tell what he's seen. Everybody has to die. If we kill a lot of them, there will no time to bury the bodies. Anyway, the ground is frozen. The best we could do would be to cover them with snow, but animals would just dig them up."

Dumont agreed that was what the carrion-eaters would do. "So we don't bury dem, we move on. When de bodies are found, the militia will know dey have not been killed with old guns."

"If they dig out the bullets," Gatling said.

Dumont smiled. "I tink the real war will start den. But dat is not so bad. The *metis* from the north will have join us. Louis will move fast when he get de guns."

Breakfast was over and Gatling was showing the *metis* how to operate the clip-loading bolt-action Mauser rifles. Dumont translated. "You pull back the bolt, then strip the bullets in the clip into the magazine. See how I do it. Then the bolt is pushed forward and the bolt turned down. Like that. These rifles use smokeless powder, so don't be surprised if you don't see smoke. These rifles are very powerful and have a kick, but nothing like the old rifles you've been using. Now I'll tell you about the sights. . . ."

Gatling went through it three times, then asked if they had any questions. "No question," Dumont said in English. "Dey understand. Dey are excited by dis new rifle and hope plenty militia will attack."

Nobody wanted to sleep. An hour later the *metis* were still examining, loading and unloading, looking through the sights, when the man who had been sent to watch the road came skittering down the side of the ravine and spoke to Dumont. The young sentry's eyes were wide with excitement.

Dumont turned to Gatling. "They're coming in from the road, militia, big party. Baptiste did not wait to count dem. But he say a lot. Hey! We talk about dis and now it happen.

Your machine gun is ready, Gatling?"

Gatling nodded. They were about 900 yards from the road, had enough time to get set. Hampered by knee-high snow, the militiamen couldn't get there in less than 15 minutes. He climbed up the side of the ravine, kicked a foothold in the snow, and set up the gun. Dumont was pointing this way and that, telling his men where to take their positions. Their bandoliers bulged with clips. Dumont said his men would hold their fire until Gatling opened up with the Light Maxim.

"I am de general of de men, but you are de general of de machine gun," Dumont said with a ferocious smile.

The colonel had been right after all, Gatling thought. You never knew what was going to happen. He brushed snow from the barrel of the Maxim. So much for not wanting to get involved.

The trees out there were jack pines, with slender trunks that wouldn't give the militiamen much cover, and they grew far apart. A good setup anyway you looked at it, a hell of a lot better than being caught on the road in slow-moving wagons.

A cold wind blew the trees. There wasn't a sound except for the wind. So far there was no sign of the militamen. Gatling rubbed his gloved hands together and used his binoculars to scout the half mile of trees. Holding his hands over the lens, to keep the snow off, he saw them moving forward in a well-spaced line, their Lee-Medford rifles held across their chests, ghostly shapes in the drifting snow. Too soon to open fire; they had to get closer.

They must have figured it out, he thought. One of their officers had. Somehow they'd learned the *metis* were moving a big shipment of guns, traveling by night, sleeping by day. Now they were hoping to catch the *metis* snoring in their blankets, empty whiskey bottles by their sides, too drunk or lazy or stupid to post guards.

In spite of the wind-blown snow, Gatling was able to count 30 men. There could be more. But there were 30 for sure.

He looked at the eight *metis* waiting below the edge of the ravine, then he opened fire, swinging the barrel of the gun from left to right. A row of militiamen went down in the snow, dead or wounded. The *metis* opened up with the Mausers, firing fast and accurately for men who hadn't handled the weapon before. Gatling fired long, spaced bursts so the barrel wouldn't get too hot. Surprised and confused, the militiamen tried to make a fight of it, but they didn't have a chance. They were dropping all along the line.

The *metis* were firing steadily, stopping only to strip fresh clips into their rifles. Gatling had linked two cartridge belts and the Maxim was jetting lead without interruption. He saw the second linked belt move into the cartridge feed. The light gun chattered, and he held it steady with the pistol grip and the forward grip. More militiamen went down in the hail of bullets. Then suddenly those who hadn't been hit turned and ran back through the tracks they'd made coming in.

Dumont looked over at Gatling and laughed like a madman, then he clawed his way up and over the edge of the ravine. His men followed. Gatling picked up the light gun and ran after them. Dead militiamen were sprawled among the trees. Three men were behind a fallen pine, firing through the withered branches. Holding the Maxim at hip level, Gatling chopped them to bits with .303-caliber bullets. Then he moved fast to catch up with the *metis*. Gunfire was coming from all directions. Not all the militiamen were running straight for the road; some were trying to lose themselves in the woods. But they left tracks, and the metis followed the tracks. Somebody was screaming off to the left. The firing continued; there was shooting all through the woods. Gatling machine-gunned a corpse that didn't look right. The "corpse" screamed and kicked and died. The *metis* had swept past a militiaman hiding behind a rock. He raised up now and fired at Gatling. He missed and ducked back into cover. Gatling blew his head off when he raised up for a second shot.

Suddenly Gatling found himself alone. The second cartridge belt wasn't used up yet, and he ran on until he reached the road. Dumont was flat in the snow, firing at three militiamen who were shooting back from the cover of a drainage ditch. They fired at Gatling because for a few seconds he made a better target. Then he was flat behind a rock, the light gun trained on the ditch, waiting for them to show themselves. Dumont crawled over to where he was. He kissed the light gun and laughed. In the woods the firing was beginning to slacken off except for an occasional shot.

"Ah, by God we have show the bastards what de *metis* can do." Dumont stroked the polished butt of his Mauser. "What a dangerous, beautiful baby, dis rifle. But your gun, your beautiful machine gun, never have I heard a gun make such music. It make me tink of woodpecker—rat-rat-rat."

Gatling wished Dumont would shut the hell up. But Dumont was sighting in on the ditch as he talked, and he squeezed the trigger and killed a man.

"Dis gun was made in heaven and blessed by God," he said. "I would like to finish dis and get some sleep." His tone was casual. "You want to walk over dere, Gatling?"

Gatling nodded. More than a hundred rounds were still in the belt. Dumont stripped in a fresh clip of bullets, and they were ready. They stood up and walked forward through the snow. In the woods the shooting had stopped. They were only 30 yards from the ditch when a shot rang out, but the bullet wasn't fired at them. Dumont laughed and the last militiaman ran up onto the road and tried to get to the ditch on the other side. Gatling brought him down with a short burst.

In the ditch, the man Dumont shot was dying. Dumont shot him in the head. The other man had shot himself. One foot was bare. His military rifle had a long barrel. He had used his big toe to press the trigger after he put the muzzle of the rifle in his mouth. There was a ragged hole in the top of his head.

Dumont laughed. "He tink *metis* torture him if he is captured. Maybe he tink right. Now we drag bodies into de woods. De bodies freeze solid, no stink. De snow hide ever'ting for a while. Dey will find dem, but we have travel plenty mile by den. Dark will not come for six-seven hour, but I tink we take chance and move on.''

They kept to the back roads east of Regina and Saskatoon. North of Saskatoon they could travel during the day; this was *metis* country, and they made better time. The British settlers had abandoned their farms and gone south for safety. Some of the German and Russian settlers had stayed on, hoping to keep out of the war. The *metis* let them alone, although they did levy a tax of grain, beef, and horses. They also seized their weapons.

They reached the Saskatchewan River and followed it north. The river was wide and pewter-colored, still frozen over and covered with snow. Dumont said the Dominion forces would send armored gunboats up the river when the ice started to break up.

Gatling got his first look at Batoche, the *metis* capital, late on the afternoon of the ninth day out from North Dakota. What had been a small river town was now a fort. It stood on high ground above the river and was enclosed by stout log walls with double rows of sandbags piled all the way up to the firing platforms. It was getting dark and the massive gate was closed.

Metis armed with old rifles and spread out along a shallow trench challenged them when they were within 500 yards of the fort. They were passed on through, and the gate opened in front of them. Lights showed in the houses; torches in metal sconces gave off flickering light and oily smoke. Men crowded around as the wagons moved into a sort of town square and halted in front of a black-painted barn.

They climbed down and Gatling saw men there who were not *metis*. The Irish Fenians he recognized by their appearance and accents, but it wasn't so easy to place the other foreigners. Some were mercenaries, professional gunmen who had fought in range wars and Central American revolutions. Now they had a nice little war very close to home. And among all these men, *metis* or otherwise, was a spy. Gatling knew he had his work cut out for him.

Dumont put a young *metis* named Baptiste in charge of unloading the wagons. It was Baptiste who had warned them of the militiamen advancing through the woods. He looked tough and capable. Dumont gave him the weapons list and a pencil. He posted two men from the wagon crew, now armed with Mausers, to keep the foreigners away from the crate containing the handguns.

"You don't trust them?" Gatling said.

"I trust dem when I can see dem," Dumont said. "Is a temptation to steal a beautiful new pistol, so I post guards. Not such good men, some of dem. I don't mean de Irishmen. Dey drink when dey can get whiskey, but dey don't steal or bodder de women. They can fight pret' damn good, I tink."

"Do you need them?"

"Louis tinks we do. Ever' man we can get. De Irishmen get paid, but not by de *metis*. Dere money come from de United States."

"How many foreigners, in all?"

" 'Bout two hundred. Hundred and thirty Irishmen, seventy gunmen. Some of dem have the police after dem, you bet. Louis don't care long as dey fight."

They came to Riel's headquarters, a one-story log cabin. No guard at the door. Dumont knocked and they went into a smoky room with a camp bed in one corner. Riel and a portly man sat at a desk with a stack of money on it. Gatling recognized the portly man right-away: a confidence man and all-around swindler named Earl Riggs. Riggs was the curse of the arms trade.

Gatling knew Riel hadn't mentioned his name or Riggs

would have made for the door. Now it was too late to dodge off, and he stood his ground. With his smooth red face and carefully trimmed mustache, he was every lonely widow's idea of what a gentleman should look like.

Dumont told Riel who Gatling was. "He have deliver de hardware," Dumont said, glancing at Riggs. "Ever'thing."

"Good," Riel said, getting up to shake hands with Gatling. "Was it an easy trip?"

Dumont burst out laughing. "Sure, Louis. We tell you later."

Riggs was trying not to look at Gatling. Riel said, "Mr. Gatling, you and this gentleman have something in common—the arms business. I'd like you to meet Mr. Henry Beederman of Cincinnati. His father founded Beederman and Blake."

Riggs offered his hand, but Gatling didn't shake it. "Hello, Riggs," he said.

"No, no, Mr. Gatling." Riel looked over the top of his half-glasses. "This gentleman's name is Beederman. Why do you address him as 'Riggs'?"

"Because that's his real name. Isn't it, Riggs? Mr. Riel, I don't care what papers and identification he showed you. They're as fake as he is. He's a con man and a fraud. Don't give him a cent. He's been swindling people all over the country for years. His main swindle is guns, but he'll pull any swindle that looks good. He even swindled the State Guard in Minnesota."

Rigg's bland face had turned beet-red. "President Riel, I protest. I can't imagine what this man is talking about. He must be drunk or has me confused with someone else. I am a legitimate businessman respected all over the United States."

"You mean you're wanted all over the United States. Now you're working Western Canada." Gatling's coat was open, swept back behind the butt of his gun. Most con men didn't go in for gunplay, but Earl Riggs was no ordinary swindler.

If his glib tongue failed him, he was always ready to shoot his way out of a tight spot. He'd killed one man who'd recognized him from somewhere else and tried to hold him for the sheriff. And he was wanted for other murders.

Riggs glared at Gatling, the picture of affronted dignity. Riel looked from one man to the other, then at Dumont, who shrugged in a very French way. The President of the *metis* nation understood what was being said, but wasn't taking it in.

"You, sir," Riggs blustered. "I don't know who you are, but I demand an apology. If this is a joke, it's in very poor taste. I have come to Canada to conduct a business transaction with President Riel. Let me tell you here and now that your accusations are as false as your motives are transparent. In short, what you want to do, sir, is cut me out."

Riggs was up on his high horse, hanging on for dear life. Gatling was getting tired of his bluster. He hadn't come all this way to listen to a slimy crook. Anywhere else he wouldn't have wasted his time on Riggs. If people were stupid enough to be swindled, then let them. But this was different: The *metis* were up against terrible odds.

"Get out," Gatling said. "Get out *now*, you crawling son of a bitch! These people have enough trouble without you."

Later, Gatling still didn't know why Riggs had tried to draw on him. Maybe he felt he was at the end of his rope. He was well-dressed, as smooth-talking as ever, yet there was something hangdog about him, as if his confidence games were beginning to go sour. Whatever the reason, he went for his gun.

Gatling shot him twice in the chest before he got it out, and he died falling to the floor. His red face became pale almost immediately. Riel didn't move, too shocked to do anything. He looked at Gatling with astonishment. Dumont took the ivory-handled .38 Colt Lightning double-action from Riggs's holster. It was silver-plated and had cost a lot of money.

"Son of a bitch, he have nice little gun," Dumont said. "You want it, Gatling?"

Gatling said no, and Dumont put the fancy gun in his pocket. Riel was getting over the shock of having a man killed a few feet from where he sat.

"But he showed me a photograph of his factory in Cincinnati." Riel picked up the photograph from his desk. "See the names above the gate: Beederman and Blake."

Gatling looked at the photograph. "This is a doctored—faked—photograph of the Gatling Company factory. Richard J. Gatling owns it. No kin to me. I ought to know what the place looks like. I worked there at one time. There are thousands of copies of this photograph. The company gives them out as advertising."

Dumont went through Riggs's pockets and turned up a pigskin wallet, a cigar case, wood matches, an old silver watch. There was 30 dollars in the wallet. Behind the faded photograph of a plain young woman, inside the lid of the watch, was an inscription: "To my son, Earl, on his graduation from the Iowa College of Practical Engineering."

Dumont put the silver watch in a barrel marked ARGENT. The other barrel, marked OR, was for gold.

"You eat bear steak?" Dumont asked Gatling. "No more stew for a while, okay?"

They had been eating reheated stew, jerked deer meat, and hard oatcakes three times a day for more than a week. Gatling didn't care if he never saw a bowl of venison stew for the rest of his life. And that goddamned black tea!

"Bear steak is fine," he said. "Got any beer?"

"Gatling don't like tea," Dumont told Riel, who had a cup of tea on his desk.

"Is that so?" Riel said politely. "I've always found tea very invigorating."

"We got beer," Dumont said. "We have coffee, but I think it is stale. We get beer when we drive de militia out of Cudworth. Plenty barrel of beer. Ever'body like beer 'cept me."

Riel took off his glasses and began to rub his eyes. He looked as if he had a bad headache. Gatling wondered how long he had gone without sleep.

"The food, Gabriel," he said. "And take care of . . ." He pointed to the body on the floor.

Dumont went out and came back with two *metis,* who carried out the body. "Ten minutes we eat," he told Gatling. There was blood on the muddy floor and he scuffed at it with his boot. "Dat Riggs, he have some nerve, by God!"

Riel made an impatient gesture; he didn't want any more talk about Riggs. Baptiste came in and spoke to Dumont in French. Riel said, "Speak English, Baptiste. Mr. Gatling may not speak French."

"We have unload de guns," Baptiste said. "Is all check out with de list. Ever' gun she have number, so is easy. Beautiful guns! How can we lose with guns like dat."

Dumont placed a huge hand on Baptiste's shoulder. "Now I have anudder 'portant mission for you. See what is happening to de steaks and de beer."

"Sit down, Mr. Gatling," Riel said. "You must be tired. I know I'd be very tired."

Dumont turned a chair around and sat with his arms resting on the back. Riel cleaned his glasses with a handkerchief and put them on. The wind was blowing across the top of the chimney and smoke was backing up, making the room smokier than it had been.

"Mr. Gatling," Riel said. "You have saved us a great deal of money. For which we are grateful."

Gatling didn't want gratitude. "Glad to do it."

"That's all very well and good, but I was about to give that man twenty-five thousand dollars in American dollars and British pounds. He suggested very forcefully that I pay the entire amount in advance, but I am not a complete fool."

Gatling grunted. Riel was foolish enough. Nobody paid in advance for undelivered goods, not even guns. Riggs was so brazen he hadn't even brought a few samples.

Dumont didn't like to hear his leader criticizing himself. "You are not a fool, Louis. You are an honest man, not a businessman. Your life have not prepare you for a man like dat."

"He was offended when I offered to pay half in advance," Riel continued. "He said his reputation would suffer if his business associates heard that I didn't trust him completely. Finally he said he would break his own long-standing rule and accept the half payment as a favor to me. He had, he said, the utmost sympathy for our cause. Once again I thank you, Mr. Gatling. The loss of so much money would have been a serious blow. Now let us put this unpleasantness behind us. I wish they'd bring the food. I'm not hungry, but I'm sure you are. Gabriel is always hungry."

"And thirsty," Dumont said. He got a bottle and a glass from a cupboard and looked at Gatling.

"I'll wait for the beer," Gatling said.

"Louis don't drink anything stronger than tea," Dumont said. He put the bottle and the glass on a table used for eating.

Two *metis* women knocked and brought in the bear steaks and a huge tankard of beer for Gatling. They set out the food, put a bowl of salt on the table, and left. Gatling took his chair over to the table.

"Dig in," Dumont said.

Chapter
FOUR

Riel looked at a map while they ate. Nobody spoke, and even Dumont was silent. Eating was serious business to the big *metis*. The bear steaks were enormous, tender and good-tasting, and Gatling drank the good Canadian beer, ice-cold from the snow. Riel looked up when they finished, and they took their chairs over to his desk.

The set-to with Riggs had kept Gatling from getting a good look at the *metis* leader. There was nothing of the Indian or mixed-blood about him, but then he was three-quarters white. He had light-brown hair, gray eyes, white man's features. Thick sideburns grew to the corner of his jawbone. He looked more French than anything else, but he didn't have a French accent when he spoke English.

He looked at Gatling. "We will move as soon as you show my men how to use the new weapons." Gatling agreed. "Gabriel will select the men you will train in the use of the Maxim machine guns and the Hotchkiss Cannons." Dumont nodded. "I don't want any of the foreigners, not even the Irishmen, to be trained in the use of the rapid-fire guns."

Gatling repeated the question he had asked Dumont earlier: "You don't trust them?"

Riel sipped his tea. "Mr. Gatling, if the hired gunmen turn on us—unlikely but possible—I want my people to have control of the rapid-fire guns. They may not win the war for us, but they will put us in a better position than we have been. A position, it is to be hoped, from which we can bargain with our oppressors."

"Why not get rid of the gunmen now? The Irishmen will back you. You didn't send for the gunmen, did you?"

"No, they just drifted in looking for work. We need all the men we can get, still do, so I agreed to hire them. Now I am not sure I made the right decision. Gabriel, while you were away, there were two unpleasant incidents."

"You mean there was trouble?" Dumont said.

"Yes. Serious trouble, I'm afraid. A *metis* from the north brought gold dust and nuggets, but it was late and I was asleep, and he decided to keep the gold until morning. During the night he was hit on the head and robbed. Nobody knows who did it."

"Son of a bitch!" Dumont growled. "I find him, you bet. What else happen?"

"Two of the gunmen got into a fight and one of them was shot in the side. He will recover. It happens that he and the man who shot him are good friends. They said they were drunk. What do you think, Mr. Gatling?"

"Run them off," Gatling said. "Do it now. They'll only get worse."

Dumont's chair threatened to collapse as he shifted his great bulk. "Gatling is smart fella, Louis. What he say is true. Get rid of dem is fine idea."

"How would you do it, Mr. Gatling?" Riel asked.

"Take their guns and horses," Gatling answered. "Chase them south. The militia will grab them or kill them, and you'll have no more problem."

"I'll consider it, Mr. Gatling."

"Did you get a letter from Colonel Pritchett? That business with Riggs—I didn't have time to ask. The colonel said he'd send the letter through O'Brien's organization."

"Yes, I got it last week. Poor Rideau. Colonel Pritchett said the two British agents who murdered him were dead. Naturally, the letter was unsigned. O'Brien's man could have been captured, the letter read. You yourself are sure they're dead."

"I'm sure," Gatling said. "I killed them." He told Riel how it had happened.

Riel said, "They dared to do that in the streets of New York. Such arrogance."

Gatling didn't say a lot worse happened in the streets of New York. "The British think they own the world. They own a lot of it."

Dumont made a spitting noise. "Dey don't own Saskatchewan, by God."

Riel took Colonel Pritchett's letter from a drawer and glanced at it. "Colonel Pritchett is certain there is a British agent in Batoche. Colonel Pritchett says the information provided by this spy murdered Rideau. We have to find him."

"It would be easier to find him if you got rid of the gunmen. Maybe it would. But he could be an Irishman or passing as one. A lot of Irishmen are in British service. He could be one of your own *metis*."

Riel looked startled. "One of my own people!"

"Why not? Men have poisoned their mothers for the insurance money. You can't vouch for every *metis* in Batoche. You can't know all of them. This man could have been sent here to kill *you*. You've got to station trusted guards at your door. Day and night. People walk in and out of here like it's a hotel lobby. This agent could come late at night, when you're alone or asleep, and kill you with a knife. Make no noise, then slip away."

Riel wasn't alarmed by the possibility. "But I have always been available to my people. Now you suggest guards and locks and bolts. The *metis* will not like it. They will think I am becoming self-important. We are simple people, have always lived a simple life. I don't like to do what you suggest, Mr. Gatling."

"But Gatling is right," Dumont cut in. "What good will we be if you are killed? I tink I am a good fighter, but I could not do what you do. I could not bargain with de British or de Canadians. I would rather kill dem than bargain with dem. Tink of dis, Louis. If peace come and we win our freedom, who will be de leader of our new government? Me? Dey would laugh at me. Boudreau? A good man but not strong enough. Charpentier? I don't think so. It have to be you, Louis. So do what Gatling says."

Riel dismissed the subject of safety with an impatient wave of his hand. "Enough advice, my friends. Guards will be posted, the door will be kept locked. Do you think I need a bodyguard when I leave the house?"

Gatling knew that was intended to be sarcastic. "Two bodyguards," he said. "That man Baptiste and another good man. That's up to Gabriel."

Dumont nodded. "I told you Gatling was smart man."

Riel brushed a speck of dirt from the map. He turned it around so they could read it. Towns and settlements were marked with red ink. Riel used the handle of his pen as a pointer. "This is Batoche. These other places are within a hundred miles of Batoche. As soon as the men are trained with the new guns, we will divide our forces into smaller forces, companies and platoons, depending on the size of the place to be attacked. Then we will move against the British who think themselves beyond our reach. Our aim will be to drive them out and gain complete control of this part of the Saskatchewan River Valley. Some of our men will be left behind to hold what we have taken."

Dumont frowned. "But not every place we take. You are tinking we will leave our men to hold only de key positions. From dere dey can control de smaller places so de settlers and de militia don't sneak back. Would take too many men to hold every'ting.''

"Exactly," Riel agreed, taking Dumont's ideas as his own. Dumont pretended to be a simple man, but Gatling knew he was anything but. Without Dumont to lead his ragtag army, Riel would be beaten hands down.

"It's vitally important that we control the country between Saskatoon and Prince Albert. North to south, approximately one hundred miles. East to west, from North Battleford to Crooked River. The same distance. All the key towns we take must be linked to Batoche by expert horsemen. If the militia or the settlers counterattack, we must know about it as soon as possible. Then we can move against them in force."

Dumont nodded. "But you are tinking maybe de militia tink dey can fool us by sending a small force to attack one town while dey are sending a big force to attack someplace else. To draw us off, try to make us send plenty man to de wrong battle. You are tinking dey don't get us dat way."

"Exactly," Riel said.

In the morning, Dumont and Gatling set about training the men. There were 400 Mauser rifles, all that Colonel Pritchett had in the warehouse and the Maxim arsenal in New Jersey. More than a thouand men, *metis* and foreign, were in Batoche, and not all the *metis* from the north had arrived.

"Chief Big Bear and his Crees will join us if he tink we are going to win," Dumont said. "Cree hate British settlers as much as de *metis* do. Dey have some gun, not enough. We could use four tousand Mauser rifle. But four hundred still ver' good. And we capture plenty Lee-Medford rifle when we take what Louis call de key positions."

"Good luck to you," Gatling said. "But I plan to head back as soon as I'm satisfied the men know how to use their weapons. That was the deal."

Dumont scratched his matted beard. "Sure, de deal. But don't you want to see how de men use dere weapon when dey fight? Colonel Pritchett, he tell Louis dat is part of de deal. He don't tell you?"

"The hell with Pritchett," Gatling said. "Let's train the men, then we'll see."

Gatling would lose 40 thousand dollars if he didn't test the new Mauser rifle in combat, as well as the new .38-caliber double-action Colt revolver, Officer's Model, with the swing-out gate. The Officer's Model would supplant the .45-caliber single-action Army Colt that had been the standard military sidearm since the '70s. He had fired the new .38 at the Maxim warehouse range. It was a well-made weapon with a smooth action, and because of the swing-out gate it was much faster to reload, but he had his doubts. The old Army single-action was heavy and dependable and had great man-stopping power. Colonel Pritchett argued that the new .38 would have as much killing power as the old .45, and more if the Army issued hollow-point bullets.

"We have to be fair," Dumont said. "We give three hundred and fifty Mauser rifle to de *metis*, fifty to de Irishmen. We don't give de gunmen nothing. Dey have dere own rifles, Winchester and Remington, and dere own ammunition. Dey come to fight, dey bring dere own weapon and dere own horse."

The bugler tried to blow them out of bed at eight o'clock, and the *metis* and the Irishmen assembled in the town square. It took longer to raise the gunmen, and it took some loud yelling by Dumont to get them out of the three newly built bunkhouses where they slept and played cards night and day. Some of them had served in the U.S. Army, or had deserted from it, and they hated discipline. Gatling knew it had to come to a showdown with these dangerous drifters.

The big double doors of the barn were unlocked, and when it came time to pass out the rifles, it would be done by Gatling and Dumont. Light snow was falling; sometimes it snowed to the end of April in this part of the country. The light was thick and would stay that way until it got dark in the early afternoon. The men, mixed-blood and outsider, huddled in their heavy coats and waited for the show to begin.

Dumont spoke to them from the porch of an old frame house. He told the metis, in French, that 350 of them would be given Mauser rifles. "I will decide who will get them," he said. A *metis* named Boulanger translated for Gatling. "I want no arguments. You may think you deserve a new Mauser, but if you don't get one, don't cry bitter tears in your morning tea. Now pay close attention. Those rifles have come thousands of miles and a good man and a loyal *metis* died for them. The man who brought them to us risked his life every mile of the long journey, and he did it not for money, but because he believes in our cause. The money was always second in his mind, and he accepts our money only because the guns do not belong to him. Those who do not get a Mauser rifle should not cry. But those who get them will cry their eyes out if just one of them is damaged."

Dumont concluded by telling them that Gatling, good friend of the *metis* nation, would speak them about their training. "Listen to him as you would listen to me." He said it in French and in English.

Gatling began by telling Major Fitzsimmons, the Irish commander, that his men would get 50 Mausers. Fitzsimmons was a florid-faced, chunky man in his middle forties, who had been a brevet major in the Civil War, and still liked to be addressed by his old rank. He was up front with Dumont's *metis* lieutenants. He interrupted Gatling with a loud complaint.

"Mr. Gatling," he bellowed. "I don't think that's fair. It's true that about half my men brought their own rifles. However, most of these rifles are cavalry carbines purchased second hand. Some are in good condition, some are not. Many of my men have been soldiers and are trained in the use of firearms. It would be a terrible waste of their fighting abilities if they weren't all armed with the best rifles available. I demand that we be given at least a hundred

Mausers."

A sea of faces looked at Gatling; he looked at the Irish major. "It's been decided," he said. "You get fifty like I said. I'm not running this show. Gabriel Dumont is. What he says goes."

One of the gunmen called out, "How come you don't call him Gineral Dumont?"

Gatling ignored him. "You hired guns don't need Mausers. You got your own hardware. Any objections?"

The same heckler yelled from the back, "Sure we do. Us boys object to being treated like niggers. Please, Colonel, sir, you got to give us a few of them Mausie rifles. We'd be mighty pleased if you did."

"No dice," Gatling said. This wasn't the place for a showdown; anyway, keeping these bastards in line, or running them off, was Dumont's business. "You'll have to make do with what you have."

Gatling got down from the porch and Dumont began to select the *metis* who were to get Mausers. He made them form a line as they were picked. Most of them were grinning. He left the Irishmen to Major Fitzsimmons.

A firing range had been set up outside the fort. Dumont told Fitzsimmons not to waste ammunition. Fitzsimmons didn't like having to take orders from a half-breed. Gatling thought the Irish major was in the wrong army. Dumont knew what Fitzsimmons was thinking, and it amused him. Dumont was a good hater, but he always spoke in a courteous manner to the arrogant Irishman.

Rifle practice went on all morning. Two days, three at the most, was all the time Gatling could give them to become accustomed to the new rifles. Riel wanted to move out on March 17th, St. Patrick's Day, a day that meant nothing to the *metis* or the hired guns. But to the Irish Fenians it was the most glorious day of the year, even here in hard-frozen

Saskatchewan. The holiday was four days away; already some of the Irish were sporting sprigs of greenery in their hats.

Looking on from the rear, Dumont winced every time a shot was fired. Every bullet fired at a target could be used to kill a militiaman, a Mounted Policeman, or a regular when the regulars finally came. But he said nothing, and he didn't interfere. He looked relieved when Gatling dismissed the riflemen and said they would continue the next morning.

On the way back to the house Dumont said, "I tink dey do pret' good."

"They did all right," Gatling said. "We'll start on the Maxims and Hotchkiss Cannons this afternoon. The Hotchkiss Balloon Gun we'll leave till we see a balloon. Got any observation balloons on you?"

Dumont laughed. "Funny man. No, we don't got balloon. How 'bout if we send up Major Fitzsimmons. Dat Irishman so full of hot air, he float right up in de sky."

"I think he's all right," Gatling said.

"Sure he's all right, as a soldier," Dumont said. "As a man he is plenty pain in de ass."

They got to Dumont's house, and he sent for steak and eggs, a lot of beer for Gatling. He drank two glasses of whiskey before the food arrived. The liquor had no noticeable effect.

Neither man spoke until they finished eating. Dumont stretched out on his camp bed and smoked a pipe. The tobacco in it was as foul-smelling as Colonel Pritchett's. For a man with so much on his mind—and Riel was not the least of his problems—he seemed at peace with the world.

Gatling stayed at the table and drank the beer. "What did you do before you became a soldier?"

"Soldier!" Dumont spoke through a mouthful of smoke. "I am no soldier, I am hunter. Since I am a boy I have been hunter. I know dis country better dan any man. I am a hunter who know how to be a soldier. Men listen to me. Dey don't do what I tell dem, I break dere ass, you bet."

"You bet," Gatling agreed.

"I can plan pret' good," Dumont said. "I can see far ahead, tink far ahead. I figure what de militia is planning to do. I do it to dem first. All dat I can do, but it don't make me a soldier."

"Sure it does. A damn good soldier, if you ask me."

Dumont turned to look at Gatling. "You don't please me to say dat. All I want is go back north and be a hunter like I was. Sometime I tink of my cabin dere and how quiet ever'ting is. No foolish talk. Nothing dere but me and de animals and de birds and de woods. I love de animals, even de wolves, even de animals I hunt. I like people, but I like more to be by myself."

Gatling was seeing another side of the *metis* commander. It didn't surprise him all that much. Big, boisterous men often had a quiet core to their nature.

"What will you do if the *metis* win their independence?"

"Go back to my cabin. Hunt."

"You don't want to be a part of Riel's government?"

"No. I told you. A hunter is all I want to be. Noting else. But if Louis and the *metis* need me I will come back. A man has to be loyal to his friends. But we talk too much 'bout me. Have you decide? Will you be wit us—wit me—when we march out from Batoche?"

Gatling didn't want to go, but he knew he would. "Why not?" he said.

During the night a *metis* woman, a widow living alone, was raped in her cabin. It was dark and she couldn't identify her attacker. She knew he wasn't a *metis* or an Irishman by the way he talked. The Irish had their own way of talking. She was sure the rapist was an American, and when he first came into the dark cabin he tried to talk nice to her. He offered her money if she was nice to him. But when she said no and tried to escape, he clamped his hand over her mouth, slapped her several times, and raped her. Then he buttoned up his pants and left, and she lay on the bed for a long time, too terrified to do anything. Finally, when the shock wore off, she came and beat her fists on Dumont's door.

Now it was morning and Riel was listening as Dumont repeated the woman's account of what happened to her. "I know her, she is a good woman and does not lie," Dumont said.

"Why didn't she scream?" Riel asked.

Gatling knew that Riel had studied for the priesthood for two years, in Montreal. He had a rich *metis* father who'd wanted his son to be a bishop someday. Riel, the failed seminarian, found it unpleasant to talk about rape.

"She is too scared to scream," Dumont said. "Maybe you tink she is a widow and misses big cock inside her? Maybe she enjoy it, den change her mind and get mad and make up dis story?"

It was the first time Gatling had seen Dumont get tough with his beloved leader. But Dumont had earned the right to talk back, although he exercised it very seldom.

"Those were not my thoughts," Riel said awkwardly. "Rape is a terrible crime, and should be punished. The woman says an American did it, but can't identify him. There are seventy Americans here. How are we to find the man responsible?"

Dumont growled, "You don't find him, Louis. I find him. Me and Gatling find him, and when he is found he don't get bullet. A bullet too good for de son of a bitch. I will hang de pig with my own hands."

Riel kept looking at the leather-bound book he'd been writing in. The pen was still in his hand. Gatling figured he wanted to get back to drafting a constitution for the *metis* nation, or something of equal importance.

"I leave the punishment to you, Gabriel." Riel wrote a

few words, but this time Dumont wasn't so easily dismissed. Riel put down his pen and sighed. "Is there something else you want to discuss?"

"Louis, I know you have many tings to tink about. But we have to talk about de Americans, the hired guns. Gatling calls dem dat, and he don't like dem no more dan I do. This attack on de woman, de trouble before dat, we have to get rid of dem. *Now*, Louis. It has to be now. We move out in a few days. Could be bad for us we don't settle dis trouble before we go. By now de *metis* know it was some American dat rape dis woman. Nobody have spoke to me 'bout it, but I know *metis* will not fight 'longside de Americans. Worse dan dat, Louis, the *metis* may try to kill all de Americans right here in Batoche. A lot of men could die for not'ing. How good we fight de militia den?"

"You think it might come to that?" Riel looked nervously from Dumont to Gatling. "What do you think, Mr. Gatling?"

"Gabriel is telling it," Gatling said. "But I agree with him. It may not come to a gun battle, but what difference does it make if it doesn't. If the *metis* don't want these gunslingers in their army, all the more reason to get rid of them."

Dumont was getting impatient again, but he got himself under control before he spoke. "Louis, you must decide before it is too late."

"Very well," Riel said at last. "Seventy professional fighters, a big loss. But you have persuaded me. I leave it up to you."

Riel's steel-nibbed pen was scratching across the page before they got to the door. Outside, Dumont socked one huge fist in the palm of his other hand. "I love Louis like a brot'er, but sometime he get me so fuckeen mad. He tink and he tink and sometime he forget what he start off to tink about. But he is our leader, he hold us together. Nobody else could do dat."

"Let's get it done," Gatling said.

Half an hour later 50 *metis* armed with Mausers escorted the American gunmen to the town square. Gatling and Dumont were on the porch of the old house. Baptiste sat behind a heavy Maxim at the top of the steps. The machine gun was just for show, and Gatling hoped they wouldn't have to use it. He would take over from Baptiste if shooting started.

For a moment it was dead quiet, and then the gunslingers began to yell.

Chapter
FIVE

They kept yelling until Gatling told Baptiste to elevate the barrel of the heavy Maxim and fire a long burst over their heads. Baptiste was the top of his class in machine-gun school. He wanted to turn the gun on the hated gunslingers, but he did what he was told.

A string of .303-caliber bullets jetted from the gun; all it took was one burst to settle the gunslingers down. Some had been in the Army and had seen the hand-cranked Gatling Gun in action, but Gatling knew nobody there had run into a fast-firing, fully automatic machine gun.

Baptiste cut loose again, though there was no need for it. Dumont told him to stop wasting ammunition. Gatling thought: Too bad he can't cut down a few trees. That would really get the point across.

The gunmen didn't have a leader. They were too thorny and independent to agree about anything. Earlier that morning, Dumont had told Gatling a tall, thin, mean-eyed Texan who called himself Jackson Manley was the closest they came to having somebody talk for them.

"It look like Manley want to talk now. Dat's him," Dumont said. "Look like goddamn stork."

Manley pushed his way through the silent crowd until he was out in front.

"That's far enough," Gatling warned him. "One more step and you get shot."

Manley, gangling and slightly round-shouldered, looked up at Gatling. He had ginger hair and his sun-browned face was dotted with dark freckles.

"You mind telling me what the hell is going on?" Manley raised his left hand to point at the Maxim gun. He was barely in control of his temper. "Why is that fucking thing pointed at us? What have we done makes you treat us like shit? These . . . these *mestizos* come banging in on us with their fucking new rifles. They get the drop on us—most of us are asleep—then they march us over here like jailbirds. One American to another, are we prisoners or what?"

Manley had his Remingington .44 belted high, its butt forward. A cross-drawn artist. Gatling knew that kind of getup could be pretty fast if the shooter knew his stuff.

"Here's what it's about," Gatling said. "You boys been making trouble. Simple as that. A *metis* was hit on the head and robbed of his gold. Two dimwits got into a gunfight over nothing. One man got shot, but it could've been a woman or a child. Last night a woman was beaten and raped. It was dark and she couldn't see her attacker's face. She says an American did it. She knew he was American by his voice."

Manley's temper broke loose and he started to shout. "That's a goddamned lie." The Texas gunslinger had a booming voice for such a narrow-chested man. "This . . . this . . . *woman*, how does she know what an American sounds like? Maybe it was one of the micks that pronged her."

From behind the gun Baptiste shouted, "She know what she know, Yankee." Dumont told him to shut up.

"Who did it, Manley?" Gatling knew he might have to

kill Manley before this was over. "Listen to me. I don't take you for a man that would shield a woman-beating rapist." Gatling knew Manley was capable of any outrage, but an appeal to the bastard's pride might get some results.

It didn't. Either Manley didn't know, or wouldn't tell. "I never beat or raped a woman in my life. Where I come from, we treat women with respect. I don't have to tear the drawers off women to get a poke. They take them off themself, and are glad to do it."

The son of a bitch was swell-headed as well as stupid, Gatling thought. "There's a hundred dollars in it for you," Gatling said. "Give me the man's name, and nobody will think less of you for doing it. The men will back you, is what I think. No decent man can stomach a sneaking, night-crawling rapist."

Manley said angrily, "I'm telling you I don't know."

"Would you tell me if you did know?"

"I guess not. Word got out I did that I'd be a marked man ever' place I went. Anyhow, I don't know a thing."

Gatling ignored Manley and spoke to the crowd. "You boys just heard me offer Manley a hundred dollars for information. Anybody want to make a hundred dollars? Come on, boys! Hundred-dollar bills don't grow on trees."

Nobody moved, nobody spoke, then Gatling said, "If that's the way you want it. Drop your guns or get dropped. That's it. No more talk. Don't even think of trying to make a fight of it. A hundred rifles are aimed at you, and you know what the machine gun can do. Let your guns slide and march out the gate and don't come back or you'll be shot on sight."

They earned their living with guns, and they hated to lose them. Without guns they felt naked, powerless, less than men. For one bad moment, Gatling thought they were going to make a fight of it. But when Baptiste turned the gun, making a sinister, ratcheting sound, and when the *metis* riflemen brought their rifles to their shoulders, the hardcases caved in. Guns began to drop all over the square.

Manley was one of the last to turn his gun loose, and he didn't drop it, he stooped and laid it on the ground. He was straightening up when a young gunny Gatling hadn't noticed before pointed with his left hand and shouted, "Manley raped the woman. I heard him bragging to some of his pals."

Manley's mouth dropped open, then he roared, "You lying son of a bitch! You crazy lying son of a bitch!" He reached down and tried to grab his gun. The young hardcase pulled a pocket pistol from under his coat and killed him with three bullets. Manley swayed like a tall tree in the wind, then toppled to the ground. Still holding the small-caliber revolver, the young hardcase backed away. Dumont took the gun away from him when he got up on the porch. He kept explaining himself. "I couldn't name Manley while he still had a gun. He would've killed me. I felt rotten about the woman, but I was too scared to say anything. I'm glad I killed him."

He tried to grab Dumont's arm. Dumont shook him off. "Shut your mouth, kid. Stand over dere and don't say not'ing. We get round to you later."

Grim-faced but silent, the hardcases marched out the gate under escort. They didn't get to take their horses or their money. Dumont laughed. "Dem bastards be in pret' bad fix pret' soon." The *metis* riflemen would march them a mile from the fort, then fire a volley over their heads to set them running. Gatling didn't give a damn what became of them. They were gone and the *metis* were better off without them. He knew mercenaries who were men of honor, but this bunch were rootless trash. If the militia didn't kill them—the militian weren't known for taking prisoners—they would end up serving long sentences. From what he knew of the harsh, cold Canadian prisons—where a convict was locked up fourteen hours a day, and the food was slop, and tobacco and newspapers were forbidden—they might as well be dead.

Metis were collecting the handguns that littered the square. "We take this kid to my house," Dumont said.

Gatling looked at the young man who had killed the Texas

hardcase. He looked about 23, but maybe he was older. It was hard to tell. He was an inch or two under six feet, and he had a long unlined face and wheat-colored hair worn long. No beard, no mustache. He didn't look like a hardcase, but then Billy the Kid hadn't looked like the killer he was.

He started to say, "You're not going to—"

"We decide what to do after we talk to you," Dumont said. "Better you tell de truth or we send you out and dey'll be waiting for you."

They sat him down at a table and the questioning began. He said his name was Alvah Towers, and he was 25, and he came from Bailey Island, Maine. His father was a shipbuilder and also owned a fishnet factory. Both businesses made a lot of money; his father was very well off. His father had worked his way up from the bottom and never let him forget it. He didn't like his father, and never had. His father had called him a wastrel because he drank beer and played cards with local men much older than he was.

"Go on," Dumont said.

"My father sent me to the Edgeworth Military Academy in Fairfax, Virginia. He thought the discipline would straighten me out. It didn't. I liked the military part of it, but I hated all the rules and regulations. They kicked me out at the end of my first year."

Dumont turned to Gatling. "Dis academy, is dere such a place?"

"There is," Gatling said.

"Of course there is," Towers said. "You can check. I forgot. There's no way to check. But I still have my school identification card and my membership card in the Gray Gourmets. That's an eating club. You have to be elected."

"Is that so?" Gatling said. "How long since you left the Academy? You say you're twenty-five."

"You still have these cards after six years? You must have been a lot of places in six years. Let's see the cards."

Towers took the cards from a cracked wallet and handed

them to Gatling. Both cards were dirty and dog-eared, but the name Alvah Eben Towers was plain enough. Towers frowned when Gatling put the cards in his pocket.

"What else you got in de wallet?" Dumont said. "Maybe you hide something in de lining you don't want us to see."

"What's there to hide?" Towers looked surprised. "I'm giving it to you straight. Here. Look for yourself."

Dumont slit the lining of the wallet with his belt knife. "Not'ing," he said. "He have fifty-tree dollar and not'ing else."

Towers picked up the wallet and put it in his inside pocket. "Why are you asking all these questions? I told you who I am, where I come from, what my father was."

"What about your mother?" Gatling asked.

"My mother died years ago."

"And your father? Is he still in Bailey Island?"

"No. I heard he retired."

"Who did you hear it from."

"A man I grew up with. I met him in a saloon in Amarillo. He'd joined the Army. He said he was pretty sure my father had gone back to Scotland. He was born in Scotland."

Another thing that couldn't be checked, Gatling thought. But there was nothing to say Towers was lying.

"How did you come to end up here?" Gatling asked.

"After the Academy I drifted, working any job I could find. Might as well tell you I was jailed for three years in the Huntsville Penitentiary for stealing a rifle. Somebody told me a big rancher named McCargo was hiring men to fight a range war. I didn't have a weapon, so I stole one."

"After you got out, what did you do?"

"Hired on for a range war. This time the rancher staked me. The cost of the weapons came out of my wages, but I didn't mind that. I was in business."

"More recently?" Gatling said.

Dumont said, "He come here 'bout five weeks ago. He tell me a man in Montana tell him dere will be a war here.

He ask me how much wages we pay, and I tell him. He have Winchester rifle and Colt pistol and say he know how to use dem. I tell him, okay, you can join our army, den I forget about him till dis morning."

Towers nodded. "That's how it happened. I'd like to know what you plan to do with me. You can't just run me off. I could run into Manley's friends and . . . well, you know what they'd do to me."

Dumont looked at Gatling. "I tink we let him stay a while." Gatling said he had no objections. "You, kid, I tink we put you with de Irishmen. De *metis* don't want nobody but *metis* . Okay, you kill de man dat rape de woman. De *metis* will not want you anyhow. I have to ask de Irish major if he want you. You sleep where you sleep before, in de bunkhouse. You can walk around de town, but don't be hard to find. Go on now. We have to talk 'bout someting else."

Towers stood up. "Thanks, Mr. Dumont. You too, Mr. Gatling. Do I get my guns back?"

"Not yet." Dumont waved him away.

"What you think?" Dumont asked after Towers left.

"I think we may have found our British agent," Gatling answered. "His story sounds straight enough, and maybe it's too straight. I could be wrong. But you know something? I get the feeling that Manley had nothing to do with raping the woman. You saw his face when Towers said he was the rapist. If that wasn't real surprise, then the man was one hell of an actor. I think Towers got a real jolt when I ordered the gunslingers to leave the fort. He knew he had to do something that would allow him to stay on. Manley was there, talking loud, so he shot him after he put down his gun. He was betting his life that we wouldn't kick him out with the rest of them. Whoever he is, he's a quick thinker. You think I'm wrong about all this?"

Dumont shrugged one of his Gallic shrugs. "I tink maybe you got it right. One ting I don't like is dat jail sentence in . . . where is it . . . Huntsville. He wipe out three years in a few words. And he remember ever'ting so well. We ask him dis and dat and he don't have to search for de answer. Answer always on de tip of his tongue. But like you say, we could be wrong. Anyhow, we watch him like de hawk."

"Goddamn right we do," Gatling said. "Does Major Fitzsimmons know we're moving out on March 17th?"

"Course he know. I tell him. De major is all right as a soldier. He don't tell nobody. Sure as hell he don't tell Towers."

"He'll tell his lieutenants and the sergeants will hear about it one way or another. The privates will hear it last, but they'll hear it. That's how it works, especially in an outfit like that."

"Anyhow we watch Towers night and day. When we are sleeping smart *metis* like Baptiste and Etienne Boulanger will watch him. He don't do a ting we don't know 'bout. He try to sneak off and tell de militia 'bout our plan to take de towns, we catch him before he get over de wall. We catch him, we hang him."

"I wouldn't mind seeing that," Gatling said.

Gatling worked with the riflemen for the rest of the morning. In the afternoon he supervised the firing of the machine guns, five light, five heavy. At three o'clock the light was getting bad and he dismissed the men, telling them there would be one more day of practice. Dumont was in the log house when he got back there.

"Anything happen?" Gatling asked, meaning the surveillance of Towers.

Dumont shook his head. "Boulanger watch him good, but have not'ing to report. Towers don't do not'ing but take a walk, maybe tirty minutes, den he go back to de bunkhouse. Boulanger say he don't talk to nobody. Just Boulanger watch him in de daytime. When it get dark, two men watch him. I tell de men on de walls to watch real good, tonight and

BORDER WAR   67

tomorrow night. I don't say not'ing 'bout Towers."

Gatling took a strip of jerked meat from a bowl and chewed on it. It was good and salty and he filled a tankard from the barrel of beer Dumont had trundled over from the storehouse. The beer didn't freeze because the storehouse had double walls with sawdust packed between them.

"Have you told Riel?" Gatling asked.

"Sure I tell him, but he don't pay much heed to what I say. Louis don't care about danger. He say if somebody kill him dey kill him. He say to me, 'Keep up de good work, Gabriel,' and den he got back to reading his book. It don't matter. The guards will kill Towers he even gets close to Louis's door."

The beer was warm from standing in the warm cabin for most of the day. Gatling didn't care. Beer was beer. Just as long as it was wet, as the man said. The beer cut the saltiness of the jerky, and he chewed more dried meat and drank more beer.

Puffing on his pipe, Dumont was silent for a long time. Then he said, "Maybe we should just shoot him, and den we have solve de problem. You don't have to shoot him, I shoot him."

"How about if we toss for it?"

"No joke, Gatling," Dumont said sternly. "Our whole plan depend on dis one man. Dat is foolish. I tink he is slippery like an eel. I tink he will find a way to escape. If dat happen our good plan go up in smoke."

"I don't think so," Gatling said. "I just decided to make him my assistant. That will free Boulanger and the others for other duty. As my assistant he'll have to stick close to me all the time. Keeping tabs on him will be my responsibility. I get the feeling he won't make his move till we're all on our way to North Battleford."

The largest *metis* force was to attack North Battleford, a sizable town about 80 miles west of Batoche. Dumont was to command this force, while smaller units of *metis* and

Irishmen attacked carefully chosen objectives. Three hundred men were to be left behind in Batoche in case of attack. Scouts were sent north and south to watch for any troop movements from Prince Albert or Saskatoon.

"You really want to kill him?" Gatling said.

"God forgive me, I do. Dis young man, he may be just what he say he is. But I feel better if I know he is dead. If Louis don't make bargain with de gov'ment plenty men will die in dis war. One more dead man, what does it matter?"

"Let him live a little longer," Gatling said. "If I catch him trying to do us dirt I'll kill him myself. Do we have a deal?"

"We have a deal," Dumont said without hesitation. "I trust you, Gatling, because you have act like a man. A word of advice from a uneducate man. Least I am uneducate in English. French, she is my language. I read plenty French book in de long, dark nights in my cabin. De more I read, de less I know 'bout men and de world. But for sure I know one thing. Do not make tings too complicate. Do not let dis Towers trip you up. My heart is sad to have to say dis. If dis Towers gets away and my men die 'cause of it, I will have to kill you. Dere would be no justice for my dead *metis* if I did not."

Gatling knew that Dumont meant exactly what he said; it didn't make him like him less. Dumont had his own way of doing things, and so did he.

Dumont knocked the ashes out of his pipe and put it in his pocket. "We eat now," he said. "I tink tonight we eat baked lake trout. Dis fish come from ver' cold lake. De icy water make de flesh firm but is tender too. You tink you like?"

"You bet I like," Gatling said.

"Too bad we don't got lemon," Dumont said.

Dumont went out to order the food, and while he was gone it started snowing again. Gatling drank beer and watched the snow climbing up the windowpanes.

Towers was lying on his bunk reading a tattered copy of the *Montreal Star* when Gatling walked into the bunkhouse at seven the next morning. It was still dark outside, and even with a kerosene lamp burning there were deep shadows in the corners of the big room. The bunkhouse stank of sweat and tobacco and gun oil. Some of the hardcases had killed time during the long idle weeks cleaning their weapons again and again.

Towers was fully dressed and he swung his legs off the bunk and sat on the edge of it. Gatling remained standing. Because they were the only ones there, the big room looked bigger than it was. There were two cast-iron stoves at either end of the room, but only one had a fire in it, and it didn't give off much heat.

Dumont said the three empty bunkhouses would be packed full of men when the *metis* arrived from the north. The space provided for the 70 hardcases would have to accommodate at least 200 *metis*.

"What's going on, Mr. Gatling?" Towers asked, folding the old newspaper.

"What makes you think something is going on?" Gatling asked.

Towers kept folding and unfolding the newspaper. What was he supposed to make of that? Gatling wondered. That Towers was just a nervous kid asking nervous questions. But he wasn't a kid; he was 25, and maybe he was older than that. Some men kept their boyish looks well into middle age.

"There's sort of a nervous feeling in the air," Towers said. "But maybe everybody is just tensed up with the war so close."

"Could be," Gatling agreed. "Now listen. I came to tell you Major Fitzsimmons doesn't want you in his outfit. He wants no criminals—that's what he called you—bunking in with his men. He'd give you a very bad time if Dumont forced you on him."

"I feel like the man without a country, Mr. Gatling. There

must be someplace I can fit in. I'd be a good soldier if I got the chance."

"You won't get it from the *metis* or the Irish," Gatling said. "How would you like to work for me? As my assistant. Can't call you an aide. I hold no rank here or anywhere else."

"What would I be doing, Mr. Gatling?"

"What I tell you to do. Anything and everything. A lot of my time goes into writing reports on the weapons my company manufactures or distributes. You could help me there. My chief is always complaining that he can hardly read my handwriting. How is yours?"

"Pretty good, Mr. Gatling. Not exactly copperplate, but nobody ever complained about it. What else, sir?"

Gatling thought he was laying on the "misters" and "sirs" a little too thick. No regular hardcase would kiss hind-end so readily. But in their way, hardcases were just like other people: They differed, one man from the other.

"Don't try so hard," Gatling said. "You'll have plenty of work when I'm ready to give it to you. One thing, though. I want you to stay close at all times. Wander off and I'll be good and mad. Remember this. I can run you off any time I choose."

"You'll have no trouble with me, Mr. Gatling. That I can guarantee." Towers paused. "Why are you doing this, Mr. Gatling?" he finally asked. "You don't know me from Adam. I never did anything for you."

"You killed the bastard that raped that woman. Things are starting to settle down. The *metis* are still angry, but they're satisfied that justice has been done. But don't start thinking they'll come to like you. They hate white Americans just a little less than they hate white Canadians. Hell! They don't even like me, and I came clear across the continent to deliver their guns."

Gatling turned to leave and Towers stood up to show respect. "Do I start today, Mr. Gatling?" Towers wanted to know. "I'm sick of sitting around here doing nothing."

"Not today," Gatling told him. "First I got to get myself organized. Hang on here a little longer. It won't kill you. But remember what I told you. When I whistle, you got to be ready to jump. No excuses, no exceptions. I'll send for you if I need you."

Gatling went back to talk to Dumont. In the morning, at first light, they were moving out.

Chapter SIX

They crossed the frozen Saskatchewan River when there was light enough to see. The river had been frozen solid for many months, but now it was just past the middle of March and the ice had thinned out a bit and there was water flowing underneath. Scouts were sent across to check the ice; they came back and said it was safe to cross. Dumont said the men left in the fort would build rafts while they were gone. The ice would start to break up early in April.

"We leave with two hundred men, but we don't come back with two hundred," Dumont said.

Two hundred men and two light wagons: one wagon for supplies, blankets, two big tents, bandages, and splints; the other for a light and heavy Maxim gun, a Hotchkiss .37-millimeter Revolving Cannon, boxes of ammunition for the Mausers and the rapid-fire guns. Gatling's modified Light Maxim was in the wagon, in a rigid-framed leather-covered case. He'd put it in there after everything else was loaded. He didn't want to have to dig for it if they ran into trouble.

Two hundred men on 200 horses; 40 remounts to be put

into service if horses died, or were killed by gunfire, or injured themselves and had to be put out of their misery. If injured horses had to be killed, it would be done with a long, old-fashioned bayonet that had been sharpened for such a purpose. Dumont said not a single shot was to be fired after they left Batoche. North Battleford, their objective, was 80 miles west, and maybe they thought they didn't have to be too careful for a good part of the journey. If they thought that, then they were goddamned fools, Dumont told them in a menacing voice. Even here, just across the river from Batoche, they were to maintain silence. Everything that could rattle had to be kept tied down. They would sleep no more than four hours a night, and they could talk then provided they talked in a whisper.

"But I want to hear sleeping, not talking," Dumont said. "And nobody has the right to ride in the wagons unless he is very sick or breaks his leg."

Away from the river they moved through low hills covered with pines. Light snow fell on the little army as it headed west. If the snow got heavier, Dumont told Gatling, the *metis* would strap on the snowshoes that hung from their saddles and lead the horses. Dumont said he thought the worst of the snowstorms were over, but the weather was as fickle as a flighty woman, and they had to be prepared for the worst. In the end, it was up to the Almighty.

Riding with the *metis* was a fighting priest everybody called Pere Mulet, which meant Father Mule in English, because he rode a big evil-tempered mule while making the rounds of his parish. The *metis* said he was as stubborn as the big animal he rode.

Dumont told Gatling about Father Mule as they rode at the head of the column. Towers, blank-faced and silent, rode beside and slightly behind Gatling. Before they left, Gatling had told Towers that he hadn't said anything the night before because Dumont had wanted the plan kept secret until the last moment. Towers had thanked Gatling for explaining that.

"Pere Mulet, he has terrible temper," Dumont said. "But Almighty God forgive him for dat. He is a saint."

"A saint with a Mauser rifle?"

"An instrument of God," Dumont said, and to him what he said wasn't a joke.

Two hours later the road came down out of the hills and they started across a wide, shallow valley with a hard north wind blowing through it, exposing the ice beneath the snow. It had been flooded before the winter freeze set in, and was now an enormous sheet of ice. They dismounted to take the weight off the horses, but it was hard work coaxing and pulling the sliding, frightened animals to the other side.

It took an hour to get across, and they mounted up again and made better time. But in places where the snow had drifted deep, they had to climb down and pull and push their horses through the drifts before they could mount up again. They had to do this time after time, but the *metis* were uncomplaining, and patient with the kicking, plunging horses.

The snow let up for a while and a pale sun gave them better light, but it remained bitter cold all through the day, and it got colder when it began to get dark. Here in this bleak country the sky was gray or dark: gray during the short hours of daylight, black by night. But sometimes at night the sky cleared and blazed with stars. This happened when it was too cold to snow, and on such nights there was a hard crust on the surface of the snow, and now and then a tree trunk split, making a sound like a rifle shot.

By seven o'clock that evening, after having traveled for 12 hours, they were 20 miles further away from Batoche. During the day, when they stopped to rest the horses, Dumont allowed them to boil their tea over small charcoal fires that were extinguished as soon as the tea was ready to drink. At night, all lights were forbidden. Any man stupid or careless enough to strike a match to light a pipe would have the hot pipe stuffed up his ass. Dumont said he would do the stuffing himself, and the *metis* believed him.

"Chew tobacco," he told them. "It's good for de digestion and doesn't make noise. One more thing, my friends. It's alright to belch if you do it like gentlemen. Put your hand over your mouths and release de air through your fingers." The *metis* laughed and Dumont said, "Not so loud. If you have to laugh, do your best to imitate de British-Canadian squires who belong to de private—No *Metis* May Apply—clubs in Regina. Say 'Ha-Ha' and let it go at dat."

Late that night, while the men were sleeping, a scout that Dumont had sent far ahead of the column came back and reported that four militiamen and a Blackfoot Indian were watching the road from the top of a high hill with brush growing up to the top and down the other side.

"Five-six miles from here," the scout said.

Dumont told the scout to wake up Baptiste and two *metis* named Pascal and Leon. They were saddled up and ready to move out in a few minutes. Dumont told Gatling where they were going. Gatling didn't offer to go with them. This was work for silent, stealthy men who could move through snow country like gray wolves; they were better at it than he'd ever be, and there was nothing to prevent Towers from slipping away if there was no one to watch him. The *metis* avoided Towers because they connected him with Manley. That was all they knew about him. They had no reason to suspect him of anything.

Dumont and the four men disappeared into a thick stand of pine trees that bordered the road on both sides. Gatling was sharing a tent with Dumont. Towers bedded down in a sleeping bag close to the tent. He was asleep now, or seemed to be, and Gatling went into the tent, covered himself with a pile of blankets, and slept. But it wasn't a sound sleep and when he woke up for the second time his watch said it was ten-fifteen. He wasn't worried about Dumont, but if anything happened to him, this expedition would fall to bits.

No longer sleepy, he went out and walked about 20 feet from the tent and stood there thinking. He was ready to go back when something struck him on the back of the head and knocked him face down in the snow. A blinding pain knifed through his skull and he fumbled for his gun and got it halfway out before it was wrenched from his hand. He staggered to his feet and saw Towers holding the gun on him. He hurled himself at Towers, but there was no strength in his body, and Towers smashed him over the head with the barrel of the Colt. He dropped like a stone.

He opened his eyes. Dumont was rubbing snow in his face. He felt as if he'd been frozen solid. "What the hell happened?" Dumont's voice was rough, impatient, angry. "Towers is gone. I see you lying dere, but first I look for Towers. I see your holster is empty, so I know he have your pistol. Your rifle is gone from the tent, and I know he have that too. Bad, Gatling. Ver' bad. Bad for you, we don't catch him. You know what time you got hit? You got hit with a rock. With dis rock."

Gatling's head still hadn't cleared. "I got hit about ten-twenty." Gatling looked at the rock in Dumont's hand. "I couldn't sleep. I looked at my watch. It was ten-fifteen. I went out and walked down toward the road. I stood there a few minutes thinking about things. Then I got hit and went down."

"How can dat happen? How can he creep up on you without you hear him? A man like you. It don't make sense, Gatling."

"He threw the rock. He couldn't have got close to me any other way. While I was down I heard somebody running. I tried to get my gun out, but he grabbed it away from me. My head cleared a bit and I went at him hard as I could. Another rap on the skull knocked me cold."

There was no sympathy in Dumont's voice. Usually Dumont put a lot of feeling into what he said. Now his voice was flat and unemotional. His anger had turned cold. "You should have made him use de gun. Fire de gun. De shot would have brought de *metis* running. They would have hang him. Now he is gone and have a three-hour start. Maybe we didn't catch him."

"Did you . . . ?"

Dumont nodded. "Yes, we kill dem with our knives. Only de Blackfoot and one man was awake. It is not important. I am going after Towers. Talk is wasting time. Get de Irish doctor to fix your head."

The Irish doctor was a denstist who hadn't had enough money to get all the way through medical school. The *metis* had no doctor, so Dumont had taken him away from Major Fitzsimmons. That left Fitzsimmons with one real M.D. and a man who had worked as a male nurse in Union Army hospitals during the Civil War.

Gatling felt the lump made by the gun barrel; his fingers came away wet with blood. But there wasn't that much blood, and except for a godawful headache he was steady enough on his feet.

Dumont called for Baptiste, and he appeared rubbing his eyes. He stared at Gatling. Dumont clicked his fingers and told him to pay attention, and he straightened up. Speaking rapid French, Dumont rattled off a string of orders. Baptiste nodded and went away, and Gatling heard the *metis* grumbling as they rolled out of their blankets.

"I have told him to get de column moving," Dumont said. "Maybe it take whole day, more dan dat, to catch up to Towers. I don't want to come back here, all dat way. Lose time. *Metis* follow my tracks. I told you go see de doctor."

Gatling didn't budge. "I don't need a doctor. I'm coming with you. It's my fault. I argued for keeping Towers alive."

"We got no time talk about dat. You want to come, okay. You don't keep up I leave you behind. You have use snowshoe?"

"Often enough."

"Okay, I see what you can do."

Towers's tracks went uphill instead of leading down to the road. Two guards were watching the road; there was a third man posted higher up at the base of a crumbling cliff. Up there they found the guard sprawled in the snow with a knife wound in his chest. Blood soaked his shirt and stained the snow. He was barely breathing. Dumont said his pulse was very weak.

"I tink he die," Dumont said. "We leave him. Dey look for him, den find him. Maybe de Irish doctor can do someting."

Gatling got a mind picture of what happened. Towers had climbed the hill, making just enough noise to be heard, but not acting sneaky. The guard had been surprised, but not too suspicious because Towers was now Gatling's man. The guard had probably asked him what he was doing out of camp, then Towers had stabbed him in the chest and left him for dead.

"Look like he have your knife as well as your gun," Dumont said.

Gatling reached down to his boot; his long-bladed knife was gone.

Towers's tracks went along the base of the cliff for about 500 yards, then turned down toward the road. He would be well past the two guards by then. On the road he would make better time.

"He don't use snowshoe so good," Dumont said, looking at the tracks that went on ahead of them. "See how he lift de snowshoe 'stead of sliding it. Will make his leg tired he don't get de hang of it. You use snowshoe all right."

"Sure," Gatling said. They didn't use snowshoes much in the States, only in the northern states that bordered the Canadian line, where there were a lot of French-Canadians. Most Americans didn't like them. Gatling had used them in northern Montana, during Army service. Some commanding officer had gotten the idea that his men could track Indians faster if they used snowshoes. The experiment had not been a success.

They moved on for five miles without talking. Then Dumont said, "Why you not want to kill Towers when I say we got to do it?"

"I thought he could be useful in some way," Gatling answered. "Then I figured it out. I thought, fill his head with false information and let him escape. After I got your approval, that is."

"What false information?"

"Like how many more guns and men were coming from the States. Large shipments of weapons, hundreds—maybe thousands—of volunteers. Not hired gunmen, volunteers. It's been twenty years since the Civil War, but there's a lot of anti-British feeling left over from it. Thinking maybe they get to grab half the country, the British would've come in on the Southern side if the North started to lose."

Pushing along fast, Dumont said, "Hey, I don't want no history lesson. I have read a book. Make de point."

Gatling said, "I think Towers might've believed the part about the volunteers. About the gun shipments? We got four wagonloads of guns through, didn't we? What's to stop other shipments? It's a long border."

"You tell Towers and we let him escape and he tell de high-ups and dey pull back troops to watch for dese volunteers and guns. Is not a bad idea. It could have cause plenty of confusion. De smart high-up would listen to Towers report, den say, 'Dey have let him escape so he can tell us dis horseshit story. I am telling you, gent'men, dis ting don't sound true. Is a plan to make us chase de wild goose. Make us send soldiers to guard the border and look for men and guns dat don't exist. So we don't do not'ing. But de rest of de high-ups, dey argue dat dey can't just do noting. Can't take de chance. De story could be true—"

"What's that up ahead," Gatling asked, cutting in. "I saw something move."

"Is a deer crossing de road," Dumont said. "Let's go. Dis plan, you would have ask me 'bout it? Okay. Den why didn't you tell me?"

"I wasn't sure it would work. Simple as that."

"Not so simple. But like I say, not a bad idea. Make no difference. Towers have escape and we have to waste time catching him. What you tink make him run off tonight?"

"Because he heard the talk about the militiamen and the

Indian up ahead. The way he figured it, there had to be other scouting parties in the area. They would get him to North Battleford.''

''And dey would be waiting for us. Gatling, is possible we don't catch dis spy. Dat fact have to be face. If we don't, I have to decide if we go on or go back to Batoche.''

They followed Tower's tracks all night. Dumont moved on relentlessly, offering no encouragement to Gatling, who hadn't used snowshoes for years. His thigh and calf muscles ached, but he'd be damned if he'd lag behind. And if he fell behind, he'd never catch up.

First light was gray and cheerless. ''See he rest dere,'' Dumont said, pointing. ''He stamp his feet, den sit down. I don't know if he have food. He could have hide some from ever' meal since we leave Batoche. I don't know if he will stop to sleep.''

Night came early; all they saw was Tower's tracks going on ahead of them. It snowed for an hour and the tracks disappeared. Now and then, Dumont stooped and brushed away the fluffy top snow with the side of his hand, uncovering the faint impression made by snowshoes.

''He don't leave de road yet,'' Dumont said. ''When he do, it will be to sleep a few hours. What bother me is he may not come back to de road. If it snow again and he leave de road, and we don't pick up de tracks, I tink we lose him.''

Morning brought more snow, so heavy that Dumont couldn't find tracks of any kind. Dumont pointed down the silent, snow-covered road. There was no movement of man or animal. Dumont said, ''De road turn and go northwest 'bout five mile from here. Towers can find North Battleford if he have compass and stay on northwest course. That would make sense. Snow will stop soon. When we get to turn in de road and dere is no tracks, den we go cross-country.''

They reached the bend in the road; snow still fell and there were no tracks to be seen. The snow let up after they were gone a mile from the road. On the far side of a high ridge, they picked up Towers' tracks.

"He is tired," Dumont said. "Moving slower dan before. De tracks are deep. He is laying his feet down heavy. Come on."

Next morning, when there was light enough to see, they climbed a long, high slope and there he was—a tiny black shape making its way up another long slope at the other side of a deep valley. Gatling uncased his binoculars and brought the climbing man in close. Towers had the Mauser slung across his back and he swayed as the high country wind pushed him hard.

"Couple of miles," Gatling said, handing the binoculars to Dumont.

Dumont used the binoculars and handed them back. "More dan a couple of miles. He look closer, de air is so clear and dere is sun."

While they were crossing the valley, climbing down and back up, Towers went over the top of the ridge without looking back. Gatling put the binoculars away. Beyond the ridge lay another valley to be crossed, another long slope that had to be climbed. The slope was so steep that Towers had taken off his snowshoes and was crawling on his hands and knees.

They were about a hundred yards up the slope when Towers sensed something that made him turn. He couldn't have heard them. There was nothing to hear. He rolled over on his back and got off one shot that smashed the stock of Dumont's rifle. Dumont was knocked back, lost his balance, and went tumbling to the bottom. He rolled over a shaley ledge and fell into a deep hole. Gatling ran and stumbled and slid down to the ledge. On the slope deep snow was threatening to become a snowslide. Dumont lay on his back with the wind knocked out of him. The snow had cushioned his fall and he struggled to his feet. He knew he couldn't get out of the hole without help.

"Idiot!" he roared. "I am not hurt. Go after him, you fool!"

Gatling started back up the slope. The snow had shifted, and was piled up in places, and it was hard to climb over it. Wind and powdered snow stung his eyes. Pale sunshine came and went as wind-driven clouds sailed across the sky. Crawling and slipping, Towers was close to the top. He turned and bolted off three shots. One came close, the others missed. Towers was crawling again, faster now because he knew how close to death he was. In a minute he'd be over the top. Gatling lay still and sighted in with the Mauser. A fierce gust of wind blew snow in his face. Some of the snow stuck to the barrel of the rifle, and he had to brush it off and sight again. Towers raised up for another shot and Gatling shot him in the chest. He rolled all the way down. The packed snow began to slide and Gatling scrambled along the side of the slope, trying to get away from it. The edge of the slide knocked him aside and he went rolling himself. He managed to stop short of the deep hole where Dumont was trapped.

Dumont had been trying to climb the shaley, crumbling walls. His gloves were badly torn. He looked up at Gatling. "Did you get de son of a bitch?"

"I got him," Gatling said. "He's buried under a mountain of snow. Throw me up your hatchet."

All the *metis* carried a small hatchet called a "trimming" hatchet. It was used for trimming the branches off small trees. The back of it could be used as a hammer. It had many uses. Its straight, sharp edge could split a skull like a melon.

Gatling chopped down a small pine, trimmed off the branches, and cut handholds in the trunk. He stuck it down into the hole and Dumont climbed after he made sure his rifle was securely in place.

He didn't thank Gatling, who didn't expect to be thanked. He took back his hatchet and stuck it in his belt. "Have to replace de stock,." he said, meaning the damaged rifle. "Too bad dere had to be shooting. Other militia scouts could hear."

"You won't find any scouts back here," Gatling said.

"There's nothing to scout back here. Scouts will be watching the road. We're a long way from the road."

"Such a cheerful man," Dumont said sourly. "Hope for de best. Look on de bright side. I hope you're right."

They got to the road and discovered that the column was ahead of them. It took them about an hour to catch up. Baptiste had been in command in Dumont's absence. He said the forward scouts hadn't seen anything. He said he had ordered the scouts to stay a mile ahead of the column.

"You hear any shooting?" Dumont asked him.

Baptiste looked surprised. "No shots. I would have told you. What is it, Gabriel?"

"Nothing," Dumont said. "You better get some sleep, Gatling. Me too. We sleep in de wagons. Are you hungry?"

"I'll eat after I sleep," Gatling said. "I'm too tired to eat."

"Tired! A big, tough man like you! How can dat be? But I will sleep too. Just so you won't feel bad. To keep you company."

Gatling slept like a dead man; beside him in the jolting wagon, Dumont snored. It wouldn't have made any difference if he'd been beating on a drum. Gatling wouldn't have heard him no matter how much noise he made.

Baptiste woke them six hours later. "Gabriel," he said. "De fort is only five miles away."

Chapter SEVEN

They moved up at five o'clock in the morning. Light wet snow that might turn to rain fell on the 200 men as they moved silently through the woods. Scouts sent on ahead came back to report that the fort had no outlying defense positions, no men in trenches or behind earthworks, but there was barbed wire staked and coiled on the slope that went up to the gate.

They had a Light and a Heavy Maxim gun, two Hotchkiss 37-millimeter Revolving Cannons. Two Hotchkiss Balloon Guns had been taken along, because they fired incendiary bullets and could be used to start fires. Dumont sent the gun crews in first, to cover the guns with oilskins after they were set up. The Maxims were water-cooled, but it wasn't cold enough for the water to freeze in the two hours they had to wait.

The riflemen were spread out in a long line, and when they were close enough the ends of the line would swing around until the fort was ringed on all sides. A second, much shorter line, would go in after the riflemen in front of it attacked the wall where the gate was. The Maxim and Hotchkiss guns would start the attack, laying down heavy fire as the first line of riflemen went up the long slope at a run. Dynamite would be used against the barbed wire.

They were in position before six. There were lights inside the fort, none in the town. Most of the townspeople had moved south, their wagons piled high with everything that wasn't too heavy to move, and now the town was deserted. Dogs were barking in the fort.

Gatling and Dumont were hunkered down in the shadows of the trees. "Sound like dey got plenty dog in dere," Dumont said in a raspy whisper. "Mountie trick, you bet. I figure we have chance to get in close in de dark. But goddamn dog betray us. Gatling, you know we have to kill ever'body in dere if dey don't give up?"

Gatling whispered back, "Maybe that's not such a good idea. There can be no peace if you do that."

"I tink so too. My idea was to capture dere guns and supplies, take dere horses and let dem go south. Den to leave a small garrison to hold de position. At first Louis agree with me, den he change his mind de night before we leave. Kill dem all if dey don't surrender when we make de attack. We give dem one chance to do dat, Louis say. I tink Louis know damn well dey won't surrender. Least de Mounties will not and dey will shame or frighten de militia into keeping up de fight."

"Too bad the Mounties are there," Gatling whispered. "I always heard they were a pretty decent bunch."

"Dey always get dere man. Now de *metis* get *dem*. But dey are ten time better men dan de militia. Dey don't kill nobody less dey have to. Mounties got plenty of nerve. Ever'body tell dem dey are de best. And brave, you bet. You know what Mounties do when we attack dere post at Duck Lake, de first days of the rebellion? Is nearly one hundred of us *metis*, six of dem. Sure dey got Winchester rifle, but dey don't got no chance. War not real war yet, so we give them chance to surrender. Den they send back word dat we are all under arrest and we better lay down our arms or de charge will be plenty serious. What can we do? We run all over dem, have to kill two men, pile on top of de others, and send dem south. Too bad dey don't stay south."

"That's their job."

"And dis is our job."

Dumont looked at the sky. Darkness was thinning out to dull gray. "Not long now, Gatling. Sure you don't want a few more guns?"

That was a joke. Dumont had stopped scowling at him since Towers's death. The guard Towers had knifed would live, so it was all right. Gatling had the Mauser slung over his shoulder, a bandolier of clips across his chest, the Colt .45 in its holster, the new Officer's Model .38 in the side pocket of his coat. And the leather case containing the modified Light Maxim lay beside him in the snow. Two 300-round belts were linked together in the feed box; all he had to do was click them into place and open fire.

"I think I got enough hardware," he whispered. "Any more and I'll sink to my knees."

It started to rain. "God does not favor de *metis* dis morning," Dumont muttered. All soldiers hated to fight in the rain. The rain came down heavier; it would turn the snow on the slope into slush. It put them at a disadvantage, but the attack had to be launched in a few minutes.

Dumont looked back at the line of *metis* riflemen waiting silently in the shadow of the trees. He fired a single shot and the Maxim and Hotchkiss guns opened fire. The Maxim loaded .303-caliber ammunition. The Hotchkiss Cannons loaded huge cartridges, ten lead balls to a cartridge. The Maxims fired automatically and were very fast-firing. The Hotchkiss Cannons were top-loaded with a feed case that held ten cartridges. How fast they fired depended on the skill and speed of the loaders. With a good gunner and a good loader, the Hotchkiss could fire 80 cartridges a minute.

Dumont started for the slope with a big heavy Webley revolver in his hand. Yelling like madmen, the *metis* riflemen hit the long slope at a dead run. Gatling couldn't run as fast because he had to carry the cased Maxim and 1200 rounds of ammunition. The ammunition belts added to the weight of the case, but he couldn't take the chance of running out of bullets. A bell was clanging inside the fort, and the riflemen cut loose after they climbed up to the firing platforms. One Gatling began to fire, and then the other. Some of the *metis* dropped as the Gatlings swept the long, bare slope with bullets.

Dumont was still ahead of his men. Gatling saw him get down on one knee, put a match to a fused dynamite stick, and throw it into the tangle of barbed wire 30 or 40 feet away. He threw another stick before the first one exploded. Then he threw a third and a fourth. The explosions were bright orange in the rain. The gunners on the wall were giving Dumont all their attention. Somehow he wasn't even scratched. Then a shell from one of the Hotchkiss guns scored a direct hit on the Gatling gun nearest the gate. The broken gun and parts of bodies were hurled into the air. Another shell tore a hole in the wall right under the hole made by the shell that killed the Gatling Gun crew. But the second Gatling was still firing. It stopped for a moment when the Heavy Maxim concentrated its fire on the firing port where the second Gatling was. Not all the barbed wire had been blown away, but there were enough holes to let the riflemen through. Fire from the walls was heavy, and the Gatling opened up again. The *metis* ran, stopped, leveled and fired, leveled and fired. Now the heavy Maxim was firing at nothing but the firing port where the Gatling was. The automatic and the mechanically operated rapid-fire guns dueled for several minutes, but the Maxim got off more bullets than the cumbersome Gatling. Screams sounded as the Gatling crew were killed by a long burst from the Maxim. The gun stopped firing and didn't start again. Two Hotchkiss shells exploded against the massive gate and it sagged on its hinges. Two more shells knocked it down. Now the two Maxims could concentrate on the riflemen on the walls. Fire from the walls was becoming weaker and the *metis* gunners started to move their weapons closer. The Hotchkiss Cannons were mounted on wheels; the Maxims were carried. The gunners took up new positions at the bottom of the slope and opened fire.

Covered by heavy fire, Dumont and his men poured through the gate. Back from the gate a cannon boomed and shrapnel tore through the front ranks of the *metis* attackers. Gatling heard Dumont shouting and knew he hadn't been killed. Holding the Light Maxim at his hip, Gatling stepped over the bodies of the dead and dying and killed the men behind the cannon with two bursts. The gate was narrow and the *metis* behind him were fighting to get through. Militiamen were still shooting from the firing platforms; others were trying to get down the ladders. Gatling raised the light gun and went through a belt and a half before everyone on the platform or climbing down from them was dead. *Metis* were coming over the back wall of the fort. Some were killed or wounded as they got over the sharp-pointed upright logs and dropped to the ground. Those behind them on the scaling ladders got over without being shot when Gatling swung the light gun and brought down the militiamen who were backing away from the wall, still firing their rifles. The parade ground was littered with bodies. Some of them were Mounties, their red coats dyed a darker red by blood. Now all the *metis* were inside the fort and the militiamen were trying to make for a low stone building that looked like an arsenal. About half of them were killed before they got to the door, but the rest got inside and began to fire their rifles from the small slit windows set into the stone.

Hand-to-hand fighting raged wherever men were too close to use their rifles effectively. The militiamen lunged with their bayonets; the *metis* fought back with their huge knives and trimming hatchets. Gatling laced the narrow windows of the arsenal with bullets. Dumont was still out in the open, and kept on firing. Gatling was down on his belly behind the light gun. The short bipod was extended and he raked the arsenal windows with bullets. He turned and saw *metis* dragging the wheeled Hotchkiss Cannons in through the gate. They turned the cannons and opened fire on the arsenal.

The arsenal door was solid oak faced with iron and it took two shells to break it in two. It still hung from its hinges. Another shell blew it into the arsenal. A fourth shell stopped the screaming and moaning that came from inside. Suddenly the fort was quiet. Gatling picked up the light gun with the bipod still extended. But there was nothing to shoot at.

The *metis* were under orders to shoot the wounded, and the crack of rifles sounded all over the fort. Some of the wounded begged for their lives. It didn't take long to get the job done. Dumont took part in the killing, his way of showing his men that he was one of them. He reloaded the Webley and walked over to where Gatling was. The rain was still coming down hard.

"It wasn't easy," he said. "We could have climbed over de walls in de dark. But de goddamned dogs . . ."

Baptiste came up and reported that they had lost 40 men. "But we killed one hundred and seventy of them. Not many rifles were in de arsenal. Some were damaged."

"Never mind de broken guns," Dumont said impatiently. "How many good guns have we captured?"

"More than two hundred rifles, Gabriel. Forty pistols, plenty of ammunition, much food, whiskey and beer, medical supplies."

"Tell de Irish doctor about de medical supplies," Dumont said.

The Irish doctor, a thin, pale-faced man about 60, was tending to the wounded *metis*. He rapped out orders to the two *metis* who were acting as his assistants. His French was

BORDER WAR

labored and his accent was bad, but they understood what he was saying. More *metis* were pressed into service. They ran to the infirmary and came back with stretchers. One by one, the wounded *metis* were carried in out of the rain.

"Forty dead. More will die of dere wounds," Dumont said. "We will leave fifty men here. Not a big force, but if Fitzsimmons and de other *metis* leaders have taken de smaller towns north and south of here, de militia will have to fight dere way back. De regular army soldiers, we must wait and see what dere commanders want to do."

Gatling had no doubt that the regulars were already on their way from the east. The Canadian Pacific ran through Lower Saskatchewan. Thousands of regulars could be rushed there in troop trains. But he said nothing, and maybe Dumont knew that he was fighting for a lost cause.

They went into a frame building the Mounties had used as their headquarters. The sergeant's office was bare except for a battered blond-oak filing cabinet, a small deal table with a scrubbed top, a few chairs. A kerosene lamp hung from a chain; a framed and tinted photograph of Queen Victoria was on the wall. On the cold cast-iron stove stood half a pot of yesterday's coffee. Any guns that might have been there had been taken away by the *metis*. It was cold and damp; the rain beat against the windowpanes.

Crumpled newspapers, kindling, and chunky logs were in a box beside the stove. Dumont started a fire and the bare room was less cold. When the sides of the stove glowed red, it was warm enough to take off their wet coats. They hung them on chair backs, to dry. When the coffee began to bubble, Dumont filled two thick, white mugs and gave one to Gatling.

The reheated coffee was bitter and black, but it was coffee. Gatling hadn't had a mug of coffee since he'd changed trains in North Dakota. Dumont would have preferred hot, sweet tea, but he drank his coffee like a man. He was behind the sergeant's desk. He started to look through the drawers and found a large brown envelope stuffed with wanted posters. He laughed as he thumbed through them. There were 50 posters: half of them offered a thousand-dollar reward for information leading to the arrest of Louis Riel, the same amount for the apprehension of Gabriel Dumont.

"Only a thousand dollar. Not much money for important *metis* like me and Louis. I keep one for souvenir, take one back to Louis. Least dey dont' say dead or alive like dey do in de States. Mounties don't like civilian killing other people for money. Course it don't make no difference if you get shot or hung. I will be honest with you, Gatling. I tink any chance of making peace with de Gov'ment have gone up in smoke. I tink they hang Louis and me if dey catch us."

"Then don't get caught," Gatling said. "Head for the border if things start to fall apart. Riel ran for Montana after the first rebellion back in '70 went bust."

"Louis won't run dis time," Dumont said.

"Then let him stay and be a martyr. You don't want to be a martyr. You wouldn't be deserting the *metis*. They won't hang or shoot the rank and file. Men like Baptiste and Boulanger may get the rope or life in prison, but they'll let the rank and file go. There will be some sort of amnesty. You have to look out for yourself."

The wet coats steamed in the heat of the stove. Dumont poured the last of the coffee into Gatling's mug. Outside, men were yelling back and forth. Wagons were being readied for the journey back to Batoche. Dumont wanted to move on as soon as possible.

Dumont said quietly, "If I want to look out for myself I stay in de north. My cabin is many days' journey from anyting. Nobody 'cept a few trappers know I am dere. Nobody bother me. No people, no war. Look out for myself. Sure I could do dat. Only I don't want to."

Gatling sipped the bitter coffee. "I shouldn't have said anything."

"No, you say anything you like, Gatling. You have done

much for de *metis*. Sure as hell I don't want to be a martyr, but I will stay to de end. Let dem hang me if—"

Baptiste knocked and came in. "Big Bear and his Crees are approaching the fort. They want to come in and talk. Is is all right?"

Dumont told Gatling what Baptiste said. "Let dem in, but watch dem. How many?"

Baptiste said it looked like Big Bear's entire tribe, maybe 300 braves. "The other Cree chiefs aren't with him," Baptiste said. "Big Bear has an important announcement to make."

Dumont got up from the desk. "Too many Indian. Big Bear and twenty of his men can come in. No more dan twenty."

They went out and Baptiste hurried on ahead of them. "Son of a bitch, they have watch de whole fight from de hills back dere. They could have help. Now we have won de battle and I tink dey want to join us. Share in de loot, maybe get guns, dat is what Big Bear want, you bet."

Big Bear rode in on an Indian pony, followed by his men. Baptiste counted 20 Crees, then ordered his men to keep the rest out. Big Bear didn't look like a bear of any kind. He wasn't even a big man; the biggest thing about him was his belly. He was about 60 and wore a thick mackinaw coat, a fur hat with side flaps, wool pants tucked into soft-leather boots. His face was flat and brown. His thick lips were unusually red. To Gatling he looked like a fat, petulant baby.

"I bid you welcome, Big Bear," Dumont said. Baptiste translated for Gatling. "Here you witness a great victory. As you can see, our enemies are all dead. You must have come a long way and must be thirsty. May I offer you a drink of beer?"

Big Bear wanted whiskey. Dumont apologized for not having any. He said the greedy militia pigs had drunk it all. "But the beer is very good. Dismount so that you may drink in comfort."

Gatling didn't think Big Bear believed the part about the

whiskey. But he accepted the beer and drank it greedily after Dumont sent a young *metis* to fetch a pitcher and a mug. Big Bear refused the mug and drank straight from the pitcher. He didn't stop until the pitcher was empty, then he shoved the pitcher at Dumont and said, "More."

"I am told you bring good tidings," Dumont said.

"I have come to join you," Big Bear said. "I have brought many warriors. You have asked me to join you many times. Now I am here." Big Bear paused to look at the new rifles carried by the *metis* and the captured Lee-Medfords being loaded into a wagon. "You will give us good rifles such as I see now."

The repeating rifle Big Bear carried was an old Henry, its butt bound with thin copper wire. A good rifle for its time, it loaded 15 rounds in a tubular magazine, but its cartridges were under-powered and it had lost out to the Winchester '73.

"I will give *you* a new rifle," Dumont said, unslinging his own Mauser and handing it to Big Bear. "This is the finest military rifle in the world. Let me show you how it works."

Big Bear wouldn't give back the Mauser and Dumont had to use Gatling's. He held up a clip, pulled back the bolt, and loaded the rifle. "See that bucket over there?" Dumont leveled the rifle and fired and and the bucket went spinning. He bolted another round and hit the bucket again. "That's how it works. Very fast, very accurate. Because we are now allies, I give you that fine rifle and all the ammunition you need."

Big Bear just grunted. Dumont saw him looking at a dead Mountie. "I want red coat and Mountie hat," Big Bear said.

The dead Mountie's tunic had two holes in it. Dumont shrugged and was about to strip it off when Big Bear spotted another dead Mountie with many bullet holes in his chest. He had been hit by machine-gun fire.

"That one." Big Bear pointed.

Baptiste said to Gatling, "He want dat one 'cause he tink other Cree chiefs will say: 'Big Bear plenty great warrior.

He have put plenty bullets in Mountie dat wear dat coat.' He will draw plenty fly to him when weather get warm."

Dumont handed the riddled tunic and hat to Big Bear, who pulled the tunic on over his mackinaw coat. It wouldn't button but he didn't mind. He stuffed the fur hat inside his mackinaw and set the dead man's hat squarely on his head.

Dumont looked on admiringly. "You look very brave," he said in the Cree language. The *metis* stood watching with deadpan faces. Gatling thought: They may be part Indian, but they've got little in common with this conceited fat man.

"Guns," Big Bear said, getting back to the subject closest to his heart. "Rifles. The *metis* are loading captured militia rifles into the wagons. The *metis* have their own rifles. Why can't my men have the rifles in the wagons?"

Dumont stood firm. "We'll talk about the rifles when we get to Batoche. No rifles till then. But we have captured much food and tobacco. We will share everything with you. Your people will say, 'Big Bear always provides for us.' "

Big Bear liked to be flattered, but he wasn't going to be put off by food and tobacco. Gatling sensed a deep antagonism between Dumont and the fat Cree. Big Bear was an easy man to dislike: vain, slippery, greedy, and not to be trusted.

"You don't share rifles," he complained as if they hadn't been through all that. He pointed to the Maxim guns and the Hotchkiss Cannons. "You think you will give us guns like that when we get to Batoche?"

"That is not possible," Dumont said patiently. "But the rifles, we will talk about the rifles in Batoche."

Baptiste whispered, "Gabriel no fool. He tink if he give rifles to Big Bear, dat fat Indian maybe try to take ever'thing. Not here in de fort but out in da woods. Ride on ahead of us, den try to make ambush. Could be plenty of trouble he do dat. Cree is not de militia."

"You don't trust Big Bear," the Indian said. "If you trust Big Bear, then give him rifles *now*."

Gatling knew Dumont wanted to take Big Bear by the throat. But Dumont remained calm. "There is no one we trust more than Big Bear. Big Bear is like a brother to us. We know the white settlers have treated the Cree unfairly. Our hearts ache for the Cree. But there can be no more talk of rifles till we arrive in Batoche. We must leave soon, my brother. It is a long journey."

Dumont left Baptiste to supervise the distribution of food and tobacco. Indians loved tobacco as much as they loved whiskey and guns. Most of the food they got was salt bacon and canned beans.

"Dat fat Cree is a son of a bitch." Dumont laughed. "I tink he eat half de food by himself. De belly he have! He look like he have twins any day now. Hard to tink de American soldiers was once afraid of him. Used to raid across de border, den run back to dis country. De Mounties put a stop to dat. He have hate Mounties ever since. He look like a fool but is sneaky, dangerous Indian. We have to watch him all de time."

Gatling asked the same question he'd asked about the hired gunslingers: "Why do you need him?"

Dumont said, "Fat bastard can keep de militia busy. Canada have no Indian wars, but Big Bear like to start one dat make him famous. Like Sitting Bull, like Crazy Horse. White Canadian don't treat Indian too bad, least not like de Americans treat them, but Big Bear don't give a damn 'bout dat." Dumont laughed. "You bet Mounties and militia will chase him pret' good when dey hear he is useful to de *metis*."

Gatling looked at the corpses that littered the parade ground. Other dead men were under the firing platforms and in the arsenal. "What're you going to do with all these bodies?" Gatling asked.

"De men we leave behind will take dem into de town in wagons. Den dey will burn de town and de bodies. Dat should do it. We don't want to start no plague. We start back as soon as de wagons are loaded. After we raise de *metis* flag."

Gatling had seen the *metis* flag flying over Batoche. It had the word LIBERTE lettered in big black letters on a white background. They raised it now; it hung listlessly in the rain. Dumont looked up at it with no expression on his face.

Boulanger approached them and told Dumont that everything was loaded. They could leave anytime. Dumont said they would leave right now.

They started back with five wagons. Three wagons taken from the fort carried the wounded and the captured weapons and supplies. It was still raining. Nearly half the *metis* force had been killed or wounded. But they had taken an important position, which was what they'd started out to do.

Dumont turned to look back at the fort; the sodden flag hung from the flagpole like a dishrag. "Maybe God isn't a Catlick," he growled. "Maybe he have no religion."

Chapter EIGHT

They traveled far into the night, bedded down for six hours, and were moving again by first light. Dumont let them have two additional hours of sleep, because they had been through a fierce fight and needed the rest. Many of the *metis* had lost relatives and friends and they were gloomy and silent. Dumont didn't want to push them too hard, but said they would have to go back to sleeping no more than four hours a night. There was always the danger of attack on Batoche. The regulars could have arrived in Saskatchewan by now, and their commanders might not wait for the breakup of ice in the river. Dumont said they had to get back to Batoche because it was the capital of the *metis* nation. It was the center of their lives and had to be defended at all costs.

At night, when they stopped to sleep, Dumont posted a heavy guard on the wagon that carried the captured rifles. It was not wise, he said, to put too much temptation in the way of Big Bear and his Crees. Big Bear sulked when he saw the guards, but there was nothing he could do about it short of a direct attack that would surely get him killed along with all his Crees.

Campfires were permitted on the way back. Night after night, Big Bear insisted on sitting at the fire outside Dumont's tent. Dumont didn't want him there, but at least they knew where he was. He complained about the food Dumont gave him but ate as much as he could get. He kept hinting that Dumont must have a bottle of whiskey hidden away. But Dumont was adamant: There was no whiskey anywhere in camp. Forced to drink beer, Big Bear drank it by the gallon, but it didn't make him crazy as whiskey would have done. But there was enough alcohol in it to make him boastful, and Dumont was subjected to endless stories about Big Bear's warlike youth. Gatling didn't know a word of the Cree language, and was glad he didn't.

One night, while Big Bear lay snoring by the fire, Dumont said, "You know what he wants now?"

"Egg in his beer?"

Dumont laughed. "I laugh because if I don't laugh I strangle de son of a bitch. No egg. He want me to make him a general in de *metis* army."

"Did you?"

"No. I told him dat have to wait till Batoche. I told him only Louis have dat authority. Den he ask me what rank I am and I tell him I am only a colonel. Even he know de difference and it please him to tink he will be higher-up dan I am. He tink about dat for a while, den he say, 'I will be a general soon, but I will give you my first order now. Which is, give me de capture rifle.' "

"What did you say?"

"I say he will be a general but in different part of de *metis* army. De Big Bear Regiment, is de name I give it. He like dat but get mad when he know he don't get de guns."

"Will you give him the guns?"

"Sure I give him de guns. De *metis* from de north are still coming, but I don't know if dey all get to Batoche. De Gov'ment will try to stop dem. So I will give Big Bear some of de capture rifles. Like I have told you, he can make enough trouble to worry de Gov'ment. Is possible other Cree and other tribe will get into de war. Some of dem may strike out on dere own. Any trouble dey make is good for de *metis*."

"What's to stop Big Bear from working for the militia after he gets the guns? The British like to hire Indians to do their dirty work. They did it during the American Revolution."

Dumont sighed. "More history lesson. Dat could happen, only I don't tink it going to happen when word is spread dat Big Bear and de Cree did plenty of killing at North Battleford. Big Bear even wear dead Mountie coat to prove he was dere."

"Who will spread this story?"

"You know damn well who will spread it," Dumont said. "I will spread it. Have it spread. Big Bear would be big fool to go near de Mountie or de militia. De Mountie would put him in irons so he could be hung legal. De militia would just hang him from a tree."

"I'm starting to feel sorry for him," Gatling said.

"Dat is a joke I know," Dumont said. "If you have any pity, my friend, save it for de white settlements Big Bear attacks. He is a cruel man but have no chance to show it till now. He will leave death and misery behind him. I would kill him myself if I didn't need him. You tink I am as bad as he is?"

"No," Gatling said. "It's the way wars are fought."

Now it was the beginning of April; it hadn't snowed for two days. The heavy rain of a few days before had turned to drizzle. There were brief intervals of weak sunshine; the country was beginning to thaw out. The water-logged road was very bad but it froze up only at night. By midday the ice turned back to mud. It was slow going, but because of the wounded, Dumont made no effort to speed it up. He set a reasonable pace and told them to keep to it.

Dr. Kane, the elderly Irishman, did his best for the wounded. Some of the wounded cried out when the wagons jolted over rough places in the road. Others bore their suffering with strained resignation. Dr. Kane dosed the worst cases with drugs and whiskey, and there were nights when he didn't sleep at all. Three of the wounded died and they buried them by the side of the road. The subsoil was still frozen and they covered the shallow graves with rocks.

Late on the following evening the camp was attacked by a large force of mounted men who came in blasting with six-shooters and ran off some of the *metis* horses. The attack was so sudden and unexpected that the raiders were gone before the *metis* could get off more than a few shots. Four men guarding the rope corral had been killed. The Indian camp hadn't been hit. Big Bear showed up wanting to know if the raiders had taken his guns. Dumont told him to go to hell.

The *metis* wanted to mount up and go after the night riders. Dumont said no. "Dat's what dey want us to do. We go on to Batoche. But not in the dark."

Later, Baptiste and two scouts found a dead man in the woods and carried the body into camp. Looking at the body, Dumont said, "So de militia play trick on us. Dey don't kill or jail de gunslingers. Dey give dem guns and send dem back to fight us. Is something I didn't expect dem to do. Now dey got not'ing to lose. De militia on one side of dem, de *metis* on de other. Pret' smart officer tink dis up, eh, Gatling?"

"Maybe a regular," Gatling said. "One thing the bastards know is night-raiding and bushwhacking. They came and went so fast, they must have good horses."

Dumont looked at the dead man. "I should have kill all of dem. My mistake. So I am not such smart man. I tink 'bout killing dem, but I don't do it. Big mistake."

Gatling said everybody makes mistakes. "My mistake was letting Towers live too long."

Dumont waved sympathy aside. "No real damage done. We kill Towers, we take de fort. Least you had good idea.

Me, I don't tink ahead. Only one more day to Batoche, but maybe take longer if dey snipe at us from de high ground. We are going to lose more men, Gatling."

"Looks like it," Gatling said.

Dumont and Gatling walked over to the Cree camp and asked Big Bear if he and his men would act as flankers. "All your men have rifles," Dumont said. "But we will give you fifty new rifles from the fort. Get between them and us, pull back if you have to. Is it a deal?"

It wasn't. Big Bear had a morning-after beer head and he was treating it with the dog that bit him. He downed a pitcher of beer, then said no. Fifty rifles were an insult. Unless his 300 men got 300 rifles, he wouldn't do it. He seemed to think he was in a strong bargaining position.

"But we didn't capture that many rifles," Dumont argued.

"The *metis* have rifles," Big Bear said. "They don't fight this time. Take rifles from them and give them to my men. They will get them back after we have killed or scared off the raiders."

Dumont was so disgusted he turned and walked away without another word. "I swear I kill dat fat Indian. Never in my life have I deal with such a sneaky, slippery snake."

Dumont rejected the idea of traveling by night; too much danger of an ambush, he said. They moved on the next morning, with *metis* flankers walking through the woods, far back from the road. Dumont pushed the column hard and the wounded suffered, but there was no help for that.

They came under sniper fire about noon; it came from a brush-covered ridge a good way back from the road. Two men were killed and one wounded. The gunmen were using long-range rifles. Dumont told his men to find some kind of cover behind the safe side of the wagons. But they had to keep moving no matter what.

The sniping stopped after the ridge petered out. It started again when the snipers found more high ground to shoot from. A wagon driver was killed. Two scouts were sent ahead to look for an ambush. Half an hour after they rode out there was heavy gunfire. They found the scouts lying dead in the road; their horses and weapons were gone.

They got to the river in the late afternoon. Batoche was on the other side; only a few lights glimmered in the half-darkness. Men were waiting with rafts to take them across. The ice was starting to break up, but there were long stretches where the ice remained solid. Dumont said the Canadian Army would have to wait a few weeks before sending gunboats.

A wide channel had been cleared so the huge rafts could get through. A thick rope anchored to stout posts stretched across the river. An overhead trolley ran along the rope; the rafts were pulled across by three huge *metis*. Dumont had posted a rear guard to hold off the guerrilla-gunmen if they attacked.

The wagons with the wounded in them went across first. Then the three rafts came back for equal numbers of Crees and *metis*. Big Bear crossed over with his men. After that, there were only 80 or 90 men to be ferried to the other shore. The Maxim and Hotchkiss guns were in the wagon with the captured rifles. The rear-guard, the last *metis* soldiers on the western side, pulled back to the water's edge and waited with Dumont and Gatling.

Gatling lay behind the Light Maxim just below the bank of the river. Dumont and the riflemen were spread out on both sides of him. There wasn't a sound except for ice cracking in the river. Gatling turned and looked at the rafts moving slowly across the wide, dark river. They were approaching the halfway point when the gunmen opened fire. Orange flashes jetted from the trees that stopped about 50 yards from the river. At the same time, dynamite exploded not far upriver. They were trying to break up the ice so it would move, trapping the rafts in midstream.

Gatling opened fire. All along the riverbank rifles cracked as the *metis* fired back at men they couldn't see. They fired at the muzzle flashes. So did Gatling. More dynamite exploded upstream. Gatling turned and looked. The fissures in the ice still hadn't reached the channel. So far the channel remained open, but for how long? Men were yelling on the rafts and on the other shore. Then there was wild cheering as the first raft got across and the men jumped ashore. The other rafts pulled in.

Heavy fire still came from the trees, but the gunmen stayed where they were, in good cover, making no move to attack. Gatling knew they would move in fast if a raft managed to come back. One final explosion sounded upriver, and then the dynamiting stopped. The *metis* stepped up their rifle fire; a raft was coming back to get them. Some of them prayed as they worked the bolts of their rifles and fired. Gatling wasn't much for prayers, but he knew how they felt. If the raft got trapped by ice, they'd all be in a bad fix. After the ammunition ran out, the gunmen would attack.

A long stretch of ice cracked with a sound like artillery. It didn't split all the way to the channel. One of the men on the raft was hit and toppled into the water and went under. The other two raftmen had to work harder to get the raft close enough so it bumped against the riverbank. They kept yelling, "Get moving! Hurry up! Jump down quick!"

Dumont yelled and the *metis* slithered down the muddy bank and threw themselves onto the swaying raft. Gatling was still firing the light gun. Dumont yelled at him. Gatling yelled back and kept on firing. Dark shapes were running from the trees. Gatling continued to fire until there was no more ammunition in the feed box. He slid down the bank and jumped onto the raft, which was starting to move. Dumont caught him before he fell.

"Idiot!" Dumont roared in French.

The gunmen got to the riverbank and opened fire. Jammed in together, the *metis* did their best to return fire. Gatling took a belt of bullets from around his neck and clicked the connector into the feed slot. There wasn't time to coil it and put it in the feed box. "Feed it in steady," he told Dumont, who slung his rifle over his shoulder. "Don't push. Keep it level and let it run through your fingers."

Gatling elevated the barrel of the gun and opened fire. Rifles cracked and flashed on the riverbank. A few *metis* went down and Dumont had his right earlobe shot away. He cursed a blue streak but held the cartridge belt steady. Three of the gunmen had been killed and lay with their heads in the water. Another burst killed or wounded others. It was too dark to say how many.

Savaged by the light gun, the hardcases flopped to their bellies in the mud. By now the raft was well out into the dark river. Gatling stopped firing and Dumont ordered the riflemen to do the same. The hardcases continued to fire, but there was nothing to aim at, and they finally gave up.

The last of the *metis* were jumping off the raft when the ice broke loose. Thousands of tons of ice buried the raft in seconds. "Son of a bitch!" Dumont roared. "We make it just in time. Tank you, God. After dis I go to confession. I go to Mass. I light candles."

They went up into the town; everybody cheered and slapped Dumont on the back. Even Gatling got slapped on the back. Big Bear and his Crees were waiting in the town square. Big Bear looked angry when he saw the captured rifles being carried into the barn that served as an arsenal. He tried to intercept Dumont and was brushed aside.

"Tomorrow we talk about ever'ting," Dumont said. "Wait. Be patient." Dumont raised his voice and shouted, "Ever'body be quiet! President Riel has a few words of praise for us. Pay attention."

Riel came out of his house following Baptiste. It was warmer than it had been, but it was cold enough, and Riel wasn't wearing a coat over his serge jacket. Under the porch lights, he looked as self-conscious as the *metis* riflemen who guarded his door. The *metis* in the square started to cheer, but choked it off when Riel raised his hand.

"You have won a great victory," he declared in a dramatic voice that was very different from his normal speaking voice. "Our oppressors have tasted *metis* steel and now lie dead and defeated. Our flag now flies above North Battleford and other key positions our forces set out to capture. This campaign has met with complete success; I am proud of you. In years to come . . ."

Mercifully, Riel kept his speech short; he concluded by welcoming Big Bear and his men to Batoche. "Metis and Cree, together we will win this war."

Big Bear was pushing forward to take a bow, but he was too late. Riel turned abruptly and went into his house. Big Bear tried to follow, but his way was barred by the sentries. The crowd started to break up.

Dumont and Gatling found Riel behind his desk reading a book. "Sit down, gentlemen," he said, waving them to chairs. "Baptiste has already made a report. Do you have anything to add to it? Forgive me, but I don't feel quite well."

Dumont glanced at Gatling, who kept his face deadpan. "Louis, did Baptiste tell you we lost forty men? Dat some of de wounded died? Did he tell you dat we were sniped at by de American gunmen we chased out of here?"

Riel nodded. "He told me. Regrettable."

"Regrettable?" Dumont gave the word another meaning. Gatling didn't know what Dumont was trying to accomplish. Maybe he expected Riel to show more interest, to give the returning *metis* a warmer welcome. Dumont was a lot older than most of his men; he pushed himself to the limit. He liked to think of himself as an iron man, but Gatling knew he was very tired.

"About Big Bear and his Cree. I am going to give dem some of de captured rifles and use dem as . . . what is de word?"

"Irregulars," Riel said.

"As irregulars. Do I have your permission to do dat?"

"Military decisions are your responsibility, Gabriel. I have told you that more than once. Now if that is all . . ."

Dumont refused to be put off. "Big Bear will torture and murder and steal. I just want you to know."

"Yes, yes." Riel picked up his book. Gatling looked at the title embossed in gold lettering on the spine. Riel was reading *Essays in Constitutional Law*.

Riel looked up from his book. "I understand what you are saying. If Big Bear's activities help our cause, then so be it. Goodnight, gentlemen."

Gatling was glad to get back to Dumont's warm house. Hot food was on its way; it felt good to pull off his wet boots and stretch out on the camp bed. Dumont drew a tankard of beer for Gatling and poured whiskey for himself. He got up to refill his glass. The fire was going good and he piled on a stack of logs. His bullet-torn ear was a bloody mess, but he ignored it.

"What's the matter with Riel? He looks sick."

"He have consumption," Dumont answered. "I get mad at him and forget he have consumption. Years ago it strike him in de lungs and it never go away. But he don't complain, so I forget he have it."

"You think he knows what he's doing? Just a question."

"Like hell just a question." Dumont was angry. "Don't ask no more question like that."

"Whatever you say. It's not my war."

That set Dumont laughing. "You would never know dat, de way you been fighting. Dat gun of yours, she is a real terror. I like de way you stay behind while de rest jump on de raft."

Gatling had nothing to say to that. It had seemed a good idea at the time.

Dumont's smile faded; he became serious. "Gatling, I tink maybe you should get out. Dat's what you told me to do. You know I can't do dat. You are different. Get out, my friend. Go back to your own country."

Gatling propped himself up on his elbow and drank beer. "Easier said than done. South of here the country is crawling with militia. We got through, but that was three weeks ago. They'll be watching the border."

"Dat is bullshit talk and you know it. You could get across. If you don't want to cross from Saskatchewan, go west to Alberta and take de Canadian Pacific to Vancouver. Cross de border dere. Nobody even look at you. You are not dat handsome."

"Sure I am," Gatling said. "You don't mind if I stay a while longer?"

Dumont gulped whiskey and smacked his lips. "Stay all you like. Your business what you do. But I tink you should go."

"Why? What the hell is eating on you?"

Dumont said, "I have bad feeling about dis war."

"Since when?" Gatling asked.

"I don't know, Gatling. It kind of build up in me. I tell you not to make things complicate. Now I'm de one dat feel complicate. Was a time I tink we could use Big Bear. Keep him under some kind of control. Always know he is a bad man, but after I listen to him talk for a week I know he is worse dan ordin'ry bad. I argue with myself. Say to myself, what difference do it make how cruel and mean he is? If he murder white settler family . . . if he murder a lot of settler family, rape dere women and girl-children, de militia have done as bad to us. Louis leave it up to me. Louis is quiet man, have never kill nobody, but he don't want to tink about tings that upset him. You understand what I am saying?"

Gatling just nodded.

"Well I will give Big Bear de rifles, not all he want, but enough to kill plenty people. I will feel bad, but I will do it. If he kill de enemy of de *metis*, den he have to be de *metis*' friend. Son of a bitch, Big Bear would kill his mother if dat would make him big cheese of de Cree nation. You mind if I don't talk about Big Bear?"

"I don't mind," Gatling said. "What're you going to do about the gunslingers?"

"Have to do something," Dumont said. "Dey know how to make war better dan de militia. Experience men. Not so easy to kill dem, I tink. Dey are worse dan de militia because nobody have control over dem. Dey fight for money, anything dey can steal. I tink dey kill and rob settler family if dey tink dey don't get caught at it. De *metis* get the blame.

It get into de newspaper dat *metis* is a bloodstain savage. All Canada, one end to de other, hate de *metis* . Kill all chance to make fair peace with Gov'ment.''

"There won't be any fair peace," Gatling said quietly. "None at all. They won't settle for anything but your unconditional surrender. The best the *metis* can hope for is some kind of self-rule under the Canadian flag. It's doubtful the Government will go that far, but there's always a chance. But it won't even be considered till long after the war."

Dumont thought for a while. "Self-rule would be better dan not'ing. All de *metis* want is to live like a free men. But Louis will never agree to self-rule. He want an independent *metis* nation. Make our own laws, have our own gov'ment and courts, our own soldiers and police. Louis say white Canadian must have passport to enter our country."

Gatling said, "That's not going to happen. The Canadian Government won't stand for it."

Dumont scowled at Gatling; he was angry again. "If you have decided *metis* will lose ever'ting, why do you stay? De guns have been paid for, okay. You have showed us how to use de guns. What is keeping you here?"

"I'd like to see what happens."

"Den you run if tings get too hot?"

"That's right. I'll help you all I can, but I won't die for your cause. Or any cause, if I can help it. You asked a question. There's your answer."

Dumont shrugged his indifference. "Do what you like, Gatling." Dumont went to the door, opened it, and yelled, "Where is our goddamn food?"

His temper improved after he put away two bear steaks, fried onions, and boiled potatoes. He poured whiskey into his black, sugary tea and loosened his belt.

"By God, I am not so hungry since I broke my arm and could not hunt for four week. Gatling, you got any idea what we do 'bout these American gunslingers?"

"Not right now," Gatling said. "I'll have to think about it."

Chapter NINE

Two days later the American gunmen attacked the tiny *metis* settlement at Prud'homme. The tiny place was only a few miles inside *metis* territory, but it was isolated, the road that went there was very bad, and it was of no military importance. Somehow it had managed to survive. Even the militia didn't bother with it; they had more important things to do. All that was before the renegade gunslingers swept into town and killed every man, woman, and child. They raped the women and girls as young as 12, burned the town, and rode out with 216 dollars in paper money and coins.

Gatling was in the cabin, cleaning and oiling his guns, when Dumont came raging in and made for the cupboard where he kept the whiskey. He was too agitated to sit down; instead, he paced the floor. After he told Gatling what had happened, he dragged a chair to the table and sat down.

"Dey killed ever'body, even de children," he said. "We got to do something. Most of the time, Baptiste say, dey are quartered at de militia barracks at Warman. That's where dey are when dey are not out killing and raping and stealing."

"I know that. You told me," Gatling said.

Dumont picked up his glass and drained it. "You tink your idea could work? I don't like it, but could it work?"

"I'm not sure. How can I be sure? In the end, it's all up to the priest. We haven't even talked to him."

"He'll do it if he is asked," Dumont said impatiently. "Pere Mulet is afraid of nothing. De man is a fighter. You saw him at North Battleford. Like a tiger."

Pere Mulet was the priest who rode a big mule as fierce-tempered as himself. His church was in the village of Cudworth, about 25 miles south of Batoche. Gatling's idea was to get word to the gunslingers that Pere Mulet—Father Mule in English—had tens of thousands of dollars worth of solid-gold religious objects hidden under the flagstoned floor of his church. Chalices, crucifixes, monstrances, chasubles embroidered with gold thread. Dumont had asked him how he knew all these words since he was a godless man. Gatling said he'd shared a cell with a rebel priest in Mexico.

"Does it have to be Pere Mulet?" Dumont didn't like the idea of using a priest as a decoy. "Can you not tink of somebody else?"

"There is nobody else," Gatling said, pushing his weapons to one side. "We can't go. Baptiste and Boulanger can't go. You want to send some *metis* that'll fall over his feet? These bastards—most of them—aren't dumb. We send a *metis* that can't pull it off and he'll get shot."

Dumont rolled his empty glass between thick fingers; his weather-beaten face was set in grim lines. "How would it work? Tell me again."

"Here's the way I see it," Gatling said. "We've been over this before, but all right. Pere Mulet came with the *metis* from Manitoba, where he was as loved and respected as he is here. For years the *metis* have been bringing him gold from the diggings in the north. During the days of peace, Pere Mulet had this raw gold made into various sacred objects worth a huge amount of money. But with the coming of war, as war approached, he hid all this gold to keep it from being stolen or confiscated. Same difference. Recently the *metis* leaders, you included, have been putting pressure on him to tell where the gold is. Good Catholics though they are, they want to sell the gold and buy much-needed weapons. The *metis* leaders place a guard over the church so Pere Mulet can't make off with the gold. They are certain the gold is somewhere in the church, but they stop short of tearing it apart. Pere Mulet is desperate. What can he do?''

"What? Don't ask me question. Tell me."

"You wanted it spelled out. I'm spelling it out." Dumont could be an exasperating man when he put his mind to it. "Pere Mulet doesn't want to lose these scared objects, but there is nobody he can turn to for help. He's a *metis* and hates the militia. He thinks of the Americans who have been run out of Batoche. Pere Mulet is a good priest but a foolish man. He thinks he can make a deal with these men. You must remember he's desperate. Pokes of gold dust are hidden with the sacred objects, he tells them. Thousands of dollars in raw gold. They can have it all if they will see him safely to the border. Naturally they plan to take everything."

Dumont got up to get whiskey. Back at the table he said, "I don't tink I would be fooled by a story like dat."

"That's because your not a greedy man. Money or gold doesn't mean much to you, does it?"

"Me? I don't give a shit about gold. I know where gold is in de North Country. Never have I said a word about it. Talk like dat bring ever' gold-crazy bastard in Canada. I dig and pan plenty gold before Louis start dis rebellion. I gave it to Louis. It was my gold dat paid for de guns you brought."

"These hardcases would think you were crazy," Gatling said. "You know why they're gunmen? Because they're lazy and don't want to work. But mostly they're greedy. Not a day they don't think about striking it rich. They think of Jesse James and they drool. They can't walk past a bank without getting a bone in their pants."

Dumont had calmed down and Gatling went back to working on his guns. It was something he liked to do. At the moment, there wasn't much else to do in Batoche.

"All right, you have convince me dey're greedy. But what happen to Pere Mulet if dey decide to torture him? Try to make him tell where de gold is. Dey may not want to drag him all the way from dere barracks to de father's church."

"Why not? What could he do? Pere Mulet, if he agrees to go, must insist that he's the only one who knows where the gold is. They can torture him to death, but they'll be wasting their time. He won't tell."

"Dese are vicious men, Gatling. Dey could torture him because he's so stubborn. What happen? What does he do?"

"Try to endure it," Gatling said quietly.

"You can say dat. Is easy to say dat when you sit here cleaning your gun. You know what dey could do to de priest?"

"I know."

"And it don't bother you?"

"Sure it bothers me. But listen. I don't think they'd torture the priest. It would be just plain dumb if they did. Warman is no distance from Cudworth. They'd have to ride into *metis* territory, but you admit yourself you're not too strong down there. Who's going to stop them? They won't torture the priest. They'll take him along."

Dumont reached into his tangled beard and scratched. "It sound too easy, de way you tell it."

"Not so. Pere Mulet will warn the gunmen about the *metis* guarding the church. Ten good men with new rifles. They'll see some of the guards before they ride in. What they won't see is you and me, the rapid-fire guns, and a hundred *metis*. They'll ride in and we'll blow them to bits."

"And de priest?"

"He'll fall off his horse and play dead."

"And if he is killed by one side or de other?"

"Then he won't have to pretend."

"It still bothers me, dis plan," Dumont said. "Maybe

some of dese bastards know we call him de fighting priest of Batoche."

"Could be," Gatling said. "But not likely. From what I saw of them, the gunslingers kept pretty much to themselves. I never saw him dressed as a priest. I didn't know he was a priest until you told me. If by chance they do know him as the fighting padre, all he can say is the Church comes before any cause. Now listen. We've been over this twice. I don't want to go over it again. What do you say?"

"I say stay where you are. I find Pere Mulet and de tree of us talk."

They had been waiting for more than a day. In spite of its name, Cudworth was a *metis* town, named after a hero of the first rebellion who had an English father. The big stone church dominated the town, which looked much like any *metis* town between Saskatoon and Prince Albert. Most of the houses were long cabins, though there were a few two-story frame houses built by *metis* merchants who had done well for themselves.

The doors of the church were closed; two *metis* riflemen guarded the entrance. Behind the doors the Heavy Maxim had been set up, with a gunner and a loader. The doors opened out. The two men standing guard would throw the doors open and take cover in the church as soon as the gunslingers rode into the town square. Then the man behind the Maxim would open fire, sweeping the town square with bullets. The gun and the gun crew were protected by sandbags.

Dumont had evacuated the town, sending everybody north to Batoche. They had strict orders to stay there, because from here on in, the town would become a target for the militia. Twenty of Dumont's men were to replace the townspeople. The blacksmith had to be hammering away when the gunmen scouted the town; places of business had to be open, and they had to have people in them. There had to be a few people in the street.

The other *metis* riflemen were in position; Dumont had placed every man himself. If they moved from where they'd been put, they would answer to him. Men were on the roof of the church, and in the bell tower. The Light Maxim was set up in a stand of pine beside the road that came in from Warman. If anybody survived, the light gun would get them as they tried to escape.

One Hotchkiss Cannon was behind the gate of a lumber yard; the other was set up in the skeleton of a half-finished frame house. After the men and guns were in position, Dumont walked around to make sure they couldn't be seen.

He came back to where Gatling sat on a sack of grain 20 feet back from the door of a feed and grain merchant. Sacks of grain were piled up in the doorway and the modified Light Maxim stood behind them with its bipod extended. Two belts of ammunition were coiled in the feed box.

"Dey should be here by now," Dumont said. It was getting close to noon. No rain or snow had fallen since the day before. "Dey should have been here early dis morning. We timed it. If—"

"They're just being careful," Gatling said. "They're probably glassing the town right this minute. Sure they want the gold, but they don't want to die for it."

Dumont lit his pipe and smoked in silence. "Dey're coming," he said. "Some of dem are." Moving fast, he put out the fire in his pipe by dipping it in a bucket of water. He unslung his rifle and threw himself down behind the grain sacks. Gatling lay on the floor, ready to put the light gun in place and start blasting.

The only sounds came from the blacksmith's shop at the far end of town. Then the hammering stopped and it was very quiet. "Two men," Dumont whispered.

Gatling took a look. Two men were coming in from the Warman road. They wore settler clothes and rode burly farm horses. One was young, the other was middle-aged, and they sure as hell looked like what they were pretending to be. They reined in and let their horses drink at a water trough. Then, taking their time, they rode out the other end of town.

Gatling looked at his watch; 15 minutes had passed. Fifteen minutes should do it, he thought. He lifted the light gun and set the bipod on the sack of grain, pushing the bipod down hard so it would have a firm hold.

A wild Rebel yell split the air and they swept into town, filling the square with men and horses, and then the church doors banged open and the Heavy Maxim opened fire. Shells from the Hotchkiss began to land in the square, tearing men and horses apart. Riflemen aimed and fired, aimed and fired. Behind the light gun, raking the square with bullets, Gatling saw Pere Mulet throw up his hands and fall to the ground. Horses jumped over him. He didn't move. Gatling swung the light gun and knocked down men and horses. Hemmed in by guns, the gunslingers tried to make a fight of it, but it was no use. Some had their horses shot out from under them, and they tried to use the dead animals as cover. Horses ran wild, kicking and screaming in terror, trying to get away from the slaughter. Forty or 50 men were killed or wounded in the first three or four minutes. The wounded crawled in the mud; the dead lay still. The killing went on and on until the puddles in the street began to turn red with blood. There was blood everywhere. A runty gunslinger Gatling had seen in Batoche had his horse killed, but he managed to land on his feet when the animal went down. He swung up onto a riderless horse and started for the Warman road. He let out a scream when he spotted Pere Mulet running toward a wagon. He turned his horse and rode down on the priest with a lariat swinging from his hand. The loop dropped down over the priest's head and tightened around his neck. He was jerked off his feet and dragged over rocks that stuck up through the mud. Still screaming, the gunslinger turned his horse again and rode around the square, daring the *metis* to kill him. He wound the end of the lariat around the saddlehorn with a few expert twists, then raised his hat like a rodeo cowboy and screamed his defiance. He wasn't hit, he wasn't even wounded. He reached for the rope and flipped the priest over on his back. Gatling got a quick look at the priest's face. A bloody mess of broken bones and torn flesh. Gatling grabbed his Mauser and shot the crazy man out of the saddle. The horse made a break for the road, still dragging the priest. The priest hit a rock so hard he was thrown into the air. Gatling killed him with a single shot. The horse ran on with the dead priest at the end of the rope.

Outside town the Light Maxim was firing steadily; in the square there was nothing more to shoot at. The *metis* held their positions until Dumont told Baptiste to get them out of there. "Get dis town cleaned up," Dumont ordered. "It look like a slaughterhouse." What Dumont meant was, kill the wounded, get rid of the bodies.

The killing started; it took a while to get it done. They shot wounded horses that couldn't be saved. Dumont sent Boulanger out to look for the body of the priest. He came back an hour later with the body roped to the back of a horse.

"The horse wasn't hit by the machine gun," Boulanger said in French. "Father Mulet was dragged for miles. A terrible way to die."

Boulanger went away and Dumont turned to Gatling. "What made you kill the priest?"

"The way he was suffering, I had to do it. Maybe I shouldn't have. He might have lived. A few of them got away. I thought, what will they do if they get their hands on him and he's still alive?"

"You did the right ting." Dumont took the soggy pipe out of his pocket and started to clean out the bowl. It was something to keep him occupied. Gatling folded the bipod and put the light gun in its case. Dumont said, "Dere was nothing else you could do."

"That's how I figure it." Gatling snapped the catches on the gun case. "Only I didn't figure it. I just did it."

Dumont decided to bury Pere Mulet in his own graveyard, along with the five *metis* who had been killed in the fight. "Louis will be angry I don't bring de body back so it can lie in state, some kind of bullshit like dat. Pere Mulet would hate dat. De man would come back and haunt me. I don't want to be haunt by a ghost with a terrible temper. Pere Mulet don't give a shit for fancy words or brass bands. *Metis* got no brass band. But if dey have a brass band he would laugh at it. Here he live and here he die and here he be buried, you bet."

Dumont left no garrison behind when they rode out of Cudworth. The gunslingers that got away would bring the militia. They would come in force; no use trying to defend the town. The militia would burn it to the ground; burning *metis* towns was what they liked best. Maybe it could be rebuilt some day, Dumont said. But even as he said it, he didn't sound too hopeful.

They got back to Batoche late that evening. Dumont told Baptiste to report to Riel. "I don't feel like talking," he said to Gatling. "I will argue with Louis in de morning. All I want right now is a big drink of whiskey. Maybe I drink de whole bottle."

Dumont got very drunk and talked to himself half the night, but he was up and around before Gatling. After looking at his watch, Gatling said, "What're you going to do at five in the morning?"

Dumont drank the last of his hot, sugary tea. "First I will make sure de sentries are awake. Den I will walk along by de river and try to tink what I would do if I was a regular army commander. De ice is breaking up and where it remain solid dey can force a passage with dynamite and ramming. Tomorrow—I mean today—we must start to stretch de logging chains across de river. Dat will be one son of a bitch job, I can tell you."

Working night and day for more than a month, a team of

blacksmiths had been linking logging chains together. The river was wide at Batoche and the linked chains had to be long enough to stretch from one bank to the other. Pilings had to be driven deep into the mud so they wouldn't tear loose when the gunboats hit. The chains had to be stretched at just the right height. Too high, the gunboats would pass underneath. Too low, the brute force of the boats' steam engines would snap the chains like string. The chains had to be stretched across the river about three feet above deck level. When the gunboats hit, everything on deck would be wrecked. It all depended on how fast the gunboats were traveling. Dumont said he hoped they'd come at night when they were less likely to spot the chains. But he didn't think that was going to happen.

After Dumont went out Gatling got dressed and boiled up a pot of coffee with the beans he had brought back from North Battleford. He built up the fire and after he finished the coffee he went out. It was a clear, starry morning; the only movement was the sentries pacing the firing platforms. The fort had been built not dead center but sideways so the men on the front wall had a good view of the river and the country to the south. The Maxims and the Hotchkiss Cannons had been set up where they could do the most damage. Everything within a half mile of the fort—rocks, bushes, humps in the ground—had been removed. Below the fort, along the water's edge, the landings had been ripped up and the timber used to reinforce the walls.

Chevaux-de-frise, barrel-shaped sections of wood with projecting spikes, ringed the fort. Originally used in Europe as a defense against cavalry attack, they were just as effective against infantrymen, expecially when the sections were connected and strung with barbed wire. Twenty feet in front of the *chevaux-de-frise* a deep, wide trench with wooden spikes imbedded in the bottom also circled the fort. It had been literally hacked from the frozen earth by hundreds of *metis*, working with little rest and little sleep. Here and there, small gunpowder charges had been used to crack the frozen sub-

BORDER WAR

soil, but for the most part it had been a backbreaking pick-and-shovel job.

This circular trench was covered by canvas stretched tight and securely pegged. A thin coat of dirt covered the canvas. Long before it was completed, rain and melting snow had filled it with water. The man or horse that plunged into it had little chance of surviving.

Looking down from the front wall of the fort, Gatling thought that all this would stop them for a while. But only for a while. He guessed the Canadian and British force of regulars would count on gunboats to reduce the fort to rubble. As far as he knew, there were no gunboats in Western Canada, but there were armored vessels on the Great Lakes and on both coasts. They could send them to Saskatchewan on flatcars or they could convert ordinary riverboats into fighting machines. They had the resources—the money—to do anything they decided to do. Backed by the might and the money of Great Britain, the Canadian Government would hit the *metis* the way Sherman hit Georgia. At least that would be their intention; they didn't know it yet, but they were in for one hell of a fight.

Gatling knew he should get out. It wasn't his war. Just the same, he had to see it through to the end.

Late that afternoon, Gatling and Dumont were in the smithy watching the blacksmiths at work. The smiths were working as fast as they could; still, Dumont as impatient. "You'll have to work faster," he said in *metis* French. "We've got to get those chains in place."

Gatling didn't know what Dumont said, but he got the meaning.

"We can work faster, but it won't be done right," the head blacksmith told him. "What good are chains if they break? You want to get the job done faster, then do it yourself. Now get the hell out of my forge. You're in the way."

A young man Gatling hadn't seen before came into the

smithy and started to say something to Dumont. Dumont waved him outside. They walked away from Gatling and stood talking as night closed in. The young, light-skinned *metis* did most of the talking. He talked and Dumont listened. After he got through talking, Dumont asked a few questions, and the young *metis* went away.

Walking back to the cabin, Dumont told Gatling the young *metis* was one of his spies just back from the south. Dumont said he had spies in many places, men whose light skin and accents allowed them to pass as ordinary French Canadians.

"De news is not good," Dumont said. The first troop train had arrived in Saskatoon and the regulars were camped on the north end of town. More troop trains were due to arrive within a week. Canadian flags and Union Jacks were flying from practically every building in Saskatoon. Fire-eating politicians, local and national, were demanding that the "rebellious half-breed rabble" be crushed without delay. It looked like all of white Canada was up in arms."

"What about rapid-fires and artillery?" Gatling asked.

"My man say dey got plenty," Dumont answered. "He watch when dey unload dem from de train. He know de rifle but not de heavy gun. He describe dem pret' good. Dey got dem all right. He don't get to make count 'cause army policeman chase him away."

"Any activity on the river?"

"Not yet. Is quiet on de river. But I guess de gunboats are on dere way. Son of a bitch, it look like we got to fight de whole British Empire. Why do dey take such trouble to beat down a few thousand *metis*?"

Gatling knew Dumont was talking to himself; the questions he asked didn't require an answer.

Unable to get at the Government, Dumont turned his anger on the hard-working blacksmiths. "Fuckeen lazy idiots, dey don't get de job done real quick, I break dere balls. I wrap de chain around dere neck and throw dem in de fuckeen river."

"They're nearly finished," Gatling said, trying to calm him down.

"I guess you are right," Dumont said gloomily. "Goddamn chains! Getting dem across de river got to be de worst part of dis whole ting. Is a lousy, dangerous job, but it have to be done. We don't get de chains up in time, de gunboats can just sail right up close to Batoche and blow it to bits."

Gatling said nothing; there was nothing to say. But he knew that unless the gunboats were stopped, that was exactly what they would do.

Chapter TEN

Stars still glimmered in the blue-black sky when Gatling and Dumont walked down to the river. The enormous raft that was to carry the chains to the far side of the river had been constructed some distance back from the bank. It was feared that if they built the raft too close to the bank its weight might cause that section of the bank to collapse.

The raft had been built with raised sides; the chain had to be on board before it was launched. Because the riverbank was high, a slope had been dug from the front of the raft to the water's edge. The raft had been built on rollers; the launching slope was lined with tree trunks. Behind the raft a hundred hard-muscled men held the ropes that would ease the raft down into the water.

"Plenty big job," Dumont said.

There was ice in the river, but most of it had broken up and been carried downstream. Dumont wasn't worried about ice; what bothered him was the possibility that the weight of the chain would sink the raft the moment it hit the water. The river was a quarter of a mile wide, and that meant an awful lot of chain.

Pilings had already been driven deep on the Batoche side of the river. On the western shore the pilings, carried across on a small raft, were firmly in place.

"Here it come," Dumont said.

The gate was open and the first of the chain carriers came out of the fort and started down the slope. Mud slowed them down. The chain was 500 feet long; it took 50 men to carry it. When they got to the riverbank they had to carry the chain half a mile downstream to where the raft was. The men in front reached the raft and circled it, coiling the chain, laying it down evenly so the raft wouldn't be lopsided. Finally, the entire chain was on the raft.

"We will know in a minute," Dumont said. He took a deep breath and gave the signal that started the launch. Big men with sledgehammers stepped forward and belted the chocks out from under the rollers. The huge raft creaked and began to move and the men behind it put their weight on the ropes to keep it from crashing down into the river. It was still moving too fast when it hit the water, but after the first tremendous splash it floated all right, and the men on the ropes hauled it back to the bank.

They held it in place while the end of the chain was secured to the pilings. The men on the raft payed out the chain as they moved out from the shore. Foot after foot, the chain slid off the back of the raft and sank to the bottom of the river. The men feeding out the chain had to be nimble as well as strong. If a man got his hand caught in the links, he would be dragged down to his death.

Halfway across the raft disappeared into the fog and for a while the only sound was the rattle of the chain. Though nobody could see it from the Batoche side, the raft was edging closer and closer to the western shore. Then a wild cry sounded through the fog. Somebody was shouting through cupped hands. Dumont looked at Gatling and smiled. All around them people were cheering.

The raft came back and the men who were to haul the chain

out of the river went on board. Dumont and Gatling went with them. It wasn't that Dumont didn't trust the men in charge of the operation. It was just that he liked to check everything himself before he was satisfied that it had been done right.

The end of the chain snaked up over the riverbank; Dumont and Gatling took their places in the long line of sweating, heaving men. Slowly—very slowly—the chain came up from the river bottom. They moved back toward the woods as the chain cleared the surface of the river and became taut. They pulled it tighter, and when it looked right one of the links was eased down onto an enormous iron hook that had been driven into the pilings. Then the end of the chain was wrapped around the pilings that supported it, and the job was done.

Dumont was very proud of his "engineers," as he called them. Gatling had seen bridges built and tunnels dug, but he was impressed by what he had seen today. The great builders had banks and governments behind them; the *metis* made do with anything they could get their hands on. Too bad they couldn't get a square deal from somebody.

Back on the Batoche side of the river, they watched as the raft was floated downstream. A mile from the first chain, the raft would be tied up. The men who carried the second chain would have to carry it three times as far as the first one. The second chain would stay on the river bottom until the gunboats passed over it. Then the *metis* waiting on the western side would haul up the chain and secure it.

"'If de plan work," Dumont said, "de gunboats cannot go north and dey cannot go south. Dey are trapped. And den we destroy dem . . . if de chains don't break. You are tinking de same ting?"

"That's what I'm thinking," Gatling said. "If they find themselves trapped they'll fight like hell to break out. What else can they do but run in close and put their men ashore."

"Sure dey will, and de *metis* will be waiting for dem."

"They'll put them ashore under heavy covering fire,"

Gatling said. "If I were you I'd move one Hotchkiss and the Heavy Maxim down from the fort. You won't be stripping the fort. You'll still have a Light Maxim and a Hotchkiss if a separate force attacks by land."

"You tink dat's what dey will do?"

"It's standard military procedure. It's something you have to expect. I know the *metis* are good fighters, but this time they'll be facing well-trained regulars."

Early next morning, at the end of a cold, clear night, the *metis* named Boulanger reported that the second chain was in place. Boulanger was exhausted, but he looked pleased with himself.

"Gabriel," he said. "We are ready for anything."

Dumont flew into a rage. "Goddamn you," he roared. "Don't ever say dat again. Never, never say such a ting. We are not ready for anyting. Get out of here, you idiot. Put up another row of sandbags outside de front wall. Dat should keep you busy, by God!"

Boulanger protested. "Gabriel, I have not slept for two nights."

"Why should you need sleep? You are asleep when you are awake. Fine some men and start filling sandbags. And when you are finished you will still not be ready for anyting."

Dumont turned and glared at Gatling. "What are you looking at?"

Gatling knew the reason for Dumont's fist-clenching anger. He knew—had known all along—that the *metis* didn't have a chance. No matter how hard he tried to pull things together, it would make no difference in the end.

"I'm looking at you," Gatling said. "You think I should get permission to look at you. Anyway, your back was turned, so how—"

Dumont got madder. "I *feel* you looking at me. Who are you to look at me like dat. A man like you?"

Gatling knew he should go out and walk around until Dumont cooled off. He liked the man, but he could be an awful pain in the ass.

Gatling stood up. "What do you mean? A man like me?"

Dumont kept clenching and unclenching his huge fists. "Dat's what I said. A man like you. You belong to not'ing. You believe in noting. You got no wife, you got no child. I tell you dis. I would hate to be a man like you."

"Fuck you, Dumont." Gatling didn't move, but he was ready if Dumont got mad enough to try something.

"Son of a bitch!" Dumont's eyes bulged with rage. He swung at Gatling and was knocked back by a solid punch in the mouth. He spat out broken teeth and came at Gatling with his head down, like a mad bull. Gatling kneed him in the face and his head snapped back. Boring in hard, Gatling drove him back to the door with rights and lefts. He should have been out cold on the floor, but he wasn't. Gatling stomped on his foot, punched him in the belly, and he hit the door so hard it tore loose from its hinges and he sailed out and landed on his back in the mud.

Gatling looked down at him. He didn't want to go on with it. It was a stupid fight to begin with. "You want to call this off?" he said. "We're both tired and edgy."

Gatling didn't feel tired or edgy; he thought it might make things better if he said he was.

"Like hell!" To show how tired he wasn't, Dumont jumped to his feet and the fight was on again. Gatling knew this was no fight between two good friends with hair-trigger tempers. Dumont was doing his best to beat him to a pulp. He threw a hard right at Dumont's head. Dumont dodged the blow and put all his strength behind a haymaker that knocked Gatling against the wall of the cabin. Dumont grabbed him by the neck and tried to beat his head against the wood. Gatling brought his knee up into Dumont's crotch, and he howled and released his hold and danced away clutching his balls. By now a crowd had gathered; even some of Big Bear's Crees were there.

Gatling moved away from the cabin. If he had to fight Dumont, he might as well give himself room. Nothing about Dumont suggested that he was ready to let it drop. He might have if the *metis* hadn't been there. What the Crees thought didn't matter; they were outsiders and didn't count. Worst of all, some of the young *metis* were beginning to taunt him. He'd been pushing them very hard, and this was their chance to get back at him.

Slit-eyed and scowling, he came at Gatling with swinging fists. He knew how to kick and bite, but fancy footwork was beyond him. Now he growled and snapped like a mean barnyard dog. Gatling backed away, but Dumont kept coming. Then he sprang at Gatling and tried to bring him down with a body hold. Gatling dodged aside just in time and Dumont fell flat in the mud. Gatling kicked him in the back of the thigh before he could get up. But he got up and danced around on one leg until feeling returned to the other. Gatling was getting sick of this nonsense, and he moved in to finish it. Dumont threw a handful of mud in his eyes; the crafty bastard had scooped it up when Gatling knocked him on his ass. Gatling backed away, half-blind and now mad as hell. He came back at Dumont and hit him several times without doing any damage. Hitting Dumont was like hitting the trunk of a tree. He took anything you threw at him without flinching. You could knock him down, but he'd be up again before you could count to three.

Dumont tried a circling movement, and for a man so nimble in other respects, he was heavy-footed when it came to fighting. "What's the matter, Big Foot?" one young *metis* jeered. "You got lead in your ass as well as your feet?" Hopping mad now, Dumont turned his head and tried to see who was baiting him. Gatling hit him in the side of the neck with a blow he had aimed at the jaw. Dumont swung and hit hard and Gatling went reeling back. Dumont dived at his legs and they went down rolling in the mud. For a few seconds Dumont was on top, then they rolled again and Gatling was on top. It went on like that. Both of them were covered with mud and horseshit. Gatling began to black out as Dumont's thick fingers tightened around his neck, cutting off his air. He broke Dumont's hold by butting him in the face. Dumont's nose spurted blood. He got blood all over Gatling and himself. They closed again and rolled again. It would have gone on and on if pistol shots hadn't sounded close to the fort. They they heard the hollow sound of a horse galloping over the planks that had been laid over the spike-filled trench.

Gatling got up first, then reached out his hand to Dumont and yanked him to his feet. The rider galloped in through the gate. He pushed his pistol back in its holster and jumped down. For a moment he was startled by the two mud-covered figures that stood in the middle of the town square. He looked away from them and shouted, "Where is Gabriel Dumont? Somebody find Gabriel Dumont."

Bloody and muddy, Dumont stepped forward and raised his hand. "What's the matter with your eyes, boy? I'm Dumont. You've got something to tell me?"

The young rider was totally confused by Dumont's filthy appearance. Could this be the man who would lead the *metis* forces to victory? He could hardly speak until Dumont clamped a dirty hand on his shoulder and squeezed.

"Gunboats have started up the river," he said in a rush of words. "Five hours ago. I'm on the second relay. I had to ride like hell."

He tried to squirm out from under Dumont's hand, but found he couldn't move.

"How many boats, boy?"

"Three boats filled with soldiers. Heavy guns on the deck, all three of them. It was dark and they were moving slow."

Dumont let the boy go. He told Gatling what the boy said, then shrugged. "Dey are finally on dere way. What did Boulanger say? Oh, yes. 'We are ready for anyting.' Let's hope so, my friend. I feel better when I know for sure we can't turn back. We have a little time yet. Let us get cleaned up and have a drink. Oh, I forget you do not drink."

"You drink whiskey," Gatling said. "And I'll drink beer."

The Heavy Maxim and the Hotchkiss Cannon had been moved to where the second chain lay at the bottom of the river. A hundred riflemen were spread out along the bank. It wasn't light yet; there was no sign of the approaching gunboats. The *metis* knew the kind of soldiers they'd be fighting if and when the regulars stormed ashore. Nearly all of the *metis* could read, except the very old people, and though the two *metis* French newspapers published in the region carried mostly local news, the exploits of the British Army, said to be the finest in the world, got some space. The Canadian Army was modeled after the British; in *metis* minds they were one and the same.

Dumont told the men not to be frightened by bayonets. Many men who would charge headlong at riflemen in position were frightened by bayonets. Dumont said the *metis* did not need bayonets because they were such good shots. He stressed the need to make every bullet count. The British-Canadians had unlimited supplies of ammunition; unfortunately the *metis* did not. However, if it looked as if the regulars were going to overrun their position, they were to fire at will.

A scout who had ridden far downriver galloped back on a lathered horse and reported that the gunboats were indeed on their way but were moving very slowly. The gunboats had big revolving lights to show them the way. These lights, the scout said, also were used to probe the darkness on both sides of the river. There were so many soldiers on board the boats, and so many guns, that the boats were deep in the water.

"Dat's why dey move so slow," Dumont said. "Dey are afraid water will wash over de side and sink dem."

The scout went on to say that the lead gunboat had a high,

thick steel prow that cut right through solid ice in places where the river was still frozen.

"We will see if dere ice-breaker can break our chains," Dumont said.

There was fog on the river when first light came; fog often followed a clear, very cold night. It would disappear as the day wore on; right now, 20 minutes before seven, the fog lay heavy just above the surface of the water. On the far side of the river, 50 *metis* waited to pull the chain out of the riverbed after the gunboats passed over it.

Gatling knew some of them would be killed; once they were spotted, the armored gunboats would open fire. Back in New York, the colonel had told him that no Maxim guns, light or heavy, had been sold to any organization or individual in Canada, not even the armed forces. However, the colonel said, the Canadian Army and Navy had been using hand-cranked Gatling Guns for years. The Canadians were a thrifty people; they wanted value for their money; and when the Gatling was first introduced in the '60's, it was the best rapid-fire gun in the world.

Gatling and Dumont didn't talk about the fight. It had started over nothing; now it was in the past. Both men knew that they would see plenty of real fighting before the day was over. And if the regulars failed to take the fort, the fighting could go on for days or even weeks. Gatling knew it couldn't last more than weeks. No way it could continue past that point.

Dumont rejected the idea of sending another scout back down-river. They would hear the gunboats as they approached; soon after that they would see them. There was no need for scouts with the enemy so close.

They waited. The fog had been gone for several hours. Dumont looked down the line of riflemen and told the man closest to him that they were moving around too much. "Pass that along," he told the *metis*. "Tell them to find a comfortable position and not to be sticking their asses up in the air.

We've got binoculars. You think the regulars don't have binoculars?"

He turned to Gatling, who was lying behind his modified Light Maxim. "You tink they are rowing de goddamn gunboats? Or maybe pulling dem with ropes?"

"I don't know what they're doing," Gatling said. "Could be they're tied up while their scouts are scouting us. By now they know what the *metis* did at North Battleford. They know what the *metis* did to the gunslingers in Cudworth. What they're doing, I figure, is looking for a *metis* trap."

"De chains?"

"Any kind of trap. An ambush. A drifting raft or small boat loaded with dynamite. But they'd blow it up with Gatlings or light artillery before it got close. I think the trap you've made is a good one. The chains will hold no matter what they throw at them."

Dumont used Gatling's binoculars to look down the river. "Not'ing. Not a ting." He gave the binoculars back to Gatling. "Maybe dey come at night. Dey have de big lights."

"They're called searchlights," Gatling said.

"A good name for dem. Are dey as bright as dat scout say?"

"They're very bright. The darker the night, the brighter they are. If they come tonight, and it's dark, we have to shoot out those lights. We can't see them if they stay behind the lights. The lights give them a big edge. They can see us but we can't see them."

"Dey got no advantage if de chain sweep ever'ting off de deck. Men. Guns. Lights. Boxes of ammunition."

"Sure," Gatling agreed. "That's what'll happen if they don't stop short of the chain."

Dumont didn't like the sound of that. "Okay, dey don't break demself on the chain, dat don't mean dey can go back. Dey are trapped."

"Trapped or not, they'll still have their guns, the soldiers their rifles. If that happens, the only way we can sink them is with the Hotchkiss Cannon. The Maxim won't make a dent in their armor plate—"

"Christ Almighty! Look at dat!"

Miles downriver an observation balloon was rising up into the clear sky. There was no wind and the balloon ascended slowly and steadily; there was no air turbulence to blow it off course. It was anchored to one of the gunboats, probably the boat taking the lead. The riflemen saw it and were disturbed by its size. The gunboats had edged their way north without being heard.

"Dey can see dat far?" Dumont asked. "Dey are a long way off."

"They can see plenty with a naval telescope," Gatling said. "I don't know if they can see us. Things don't look the same from high up. They can see the fort plain enough. Tell the men to flatten out and hug the ground."

Dumont passed the order down the line. "You have been up in a balloon, Gatling?"

Gatling uncased his binoculars. The sun was behind him; the lenses wouldn't flash. "I was up in an Army balloon when I was trying to sell Gatlings to some general. Aberdeen, Maryland. Like I told you, things on the ground didn't look the same. The general let me use his telescope. I could see wagons moving on the roads. Very small. People were harder to see."

Gatling adjusted the screw of the binoculars; two men were in the balloon. One was looking through a telescope; the lens flashed. Up high, the balloon remained steady.

He handed the binoculars to Dumont. "Son of a bitch! I can see dem real good. One of dem have a beard. You tink you can shoot dem down with de Balloon Gun?"

Gatling took another look at the balloon. "Not from here. They'd have to be closer. The balloon rifle is seventy-caliber and carries a big load. But it won't shoot that far."

"Look! It's going back down. You tink dey will go up again?"

"I don't know. We'll just have to wait. I'm going down there and take a look."

Gatling took the Mauser because he might run into Army scouts. They would hardly tie up in *metis* country without taking some precautions. But you never knew what any military commander was going to do. Gatling had known more than a few high-ranking officers who were stupid, stubborn, and just plain crazy. Custer could have taken a Gatling Gun battery to the Little Big Horn. He left the five Gatlings at the fort because he decided they slowed him down.

He left the modified Light Maxim in Dumont's care. "Remember, it isn't water-cooled. That one is." He meant the Heavy Maxim that had been set up to cover the river. "My gun has to be fired in short bursts."

Dumont didn't like to be instructed about anything. "Please, Gatling, I have seen you firing de gun. I know how you shoot it. I will shoot it de same way."

Pine woods came down to the water's edge after Gatling had gone two miles. There was no way to tell if the men in the balloon had spotted them. It would be bad if they had; the light artillery would open fire from a distance. The Hotchkiss was a fine weapon, but it didn't have the range of a light, breech-loading, rifled cannon. They might even have big guns on board, though he didn't think so. Small gunboats—they had to be small for river warfare—weren't built to take the recoil of heavy guns.

The woods offered plenty of cover; big and small rocks were scattered everywhere; there were stunted, brush-covered hills. But what was cover for him was also cover for them. These men were regulars, and though Canada hadn't fought any recent wars, its army had a good reputation. The British influence again.

He had come about five miles when the pines began to thin out. Now he had to cross a long, wide meadow that went down to the river. The grass was frozen and yellow and lifeless-looking. The meadow was more than half a mile wide. On the far side, the woods started again.

If they were there, and if they were watching, now was the time to kill him. A marksman with a scoped Lee-Medford could hardly miss. And if he did miss, he had lots of chances left; the meadow was level and bare, the grass flattened by ice and snow. He walked with the Mauser at the ready position. He got halfway across. Nobody shot at him. They might have orders to take him prisoner. He couldn't let that happen. He'd be in for some very rough treatment if it did. The way he looked, they might take him for a *metis*, and *metis* were filthy, treacherous animals. All half-breeds and mixed-bloods were treacherous. A man could respect a full-blooded Indian; a *metis* was a stinking mongrel and hardly deserved to be called a man. Killing or torturing a *metis* was less than nothing.

The woods were dark and silent. He walked on waiting for a rifle to crack or men to pile on top of him. A few minutes later he heard something up ahead. He knew he couldn't be far from the boats. He couldn't tell what was making the sound. The sound was sharp but small; if the wind had been blowing away from him, he might not have heard it. It was repeated every two or three minutes. It wasn't being made by a small branch cracking under the weight of ice.

Gatling got down and crawled, with the Mauser in the crook of his arms. If he slung it, he might not be able to get at it fast enough. He stopped and listened. The cracking noise sounded again and he knew where it was coming from: a half-circle of rocks with brush growing between them. A good place to hide in; a good place to shoot from. The muzzle of a Lee-Medford stuck out through the brush where it was thin.

Gatling crawled away and around until he was behind the rifleman's nest. He raised up and got a good look at the soldier. He was very young, towheaded and fuzz-faced, and he was cracking walnuts. Every few minutes he reached into his greatcoat pocket and took out a nut and cracked it between two small, flat rocks. Then he chewed and swallowed and reached for another nut. He was half-turned from Gatling, but he would have been an easy kill. Gatling knew he could knife of strangle the young soldier and not make a sound. But killing like that was pointless.

Concealed by rocks, he backed away; when he was far enough away to stand up he moved down toward the river. Soon he heard voices and the throbbing of engines. He crawled to the bank of the river. He was so close, he didn't need the binoculars.

Three gunboats were moored to thick iron spikes driven into the frozen ground at an angle. The one closest to him was the biggest. Cleated gangways reached up to the riverbank. Thin smoke drifted up from the funnels of the boats. On the big boat were two Gatlings mounted on swivels. A single rifled cannon was placed forward. It stood on a circular sheet of heavy tin; the gun was bolted down, but the wooden platform under the tin could be turned by raised handles. Steel boxes painted dark green stood beside the guns: feed-cases for the Gatlings, shells for the rifled cannon. They had plenty of both.

Enlisted men were on deck and on the riverbank; others had to be below decks. They wore black uniforms and thick wool greatcoats of the same color. Bandoliers were slung across their chests. He could tell the officers by the colored tabs on their collars. The tabs were blue, yellow, red. Only four men wore red tabs. The lead boat was big enough to carry 500 men, if they packed them in tight. Together, the smaller boats would be able to handle about 600. And more gunboats, he thought, might be on their way.

The two smaller gunboats had a single searchlight placed forward. The lead boat had two; one forward, one astern. They were powered by huge storage batteries, charged and recharged by the engines. This allowed the searchlights to be used when the engines were shut down.

The observation balloon, now deflated and limp, lay on the deck of the lead boat. A hose ran from the balloon down to the engine room. The balloon could be filled with hot air and sent aloft in minutes. It was all pretty efficient.

Gatling had seen all he needed to see and he went back through the woods, keeping well away from the nutcracking soldier.

Dumont laughed when Gatling told him about the nut-loving regular. "If dere all like him, we don't got much to worry 'bout."

"Stay worried," Gatling said. Sure the kid was careless, probably because nobody seemed to feel themselves in any real danger, but he might be the best shot in his outfit.

Chapter ELEVEN

It got dark and the evening dragged on and there was mist on the river. Unless he was dead wrong, Gatling figured this was going to be a night attack. They would come upstream without lights; the gunboats were crewed by Navy men, and there would be a pilot in the lead boat. A few miles downstream they would slow their engines and creep along without making much noise. If they were lucky, no alarm would be sounded until they were right below Batoche. Then the searchlights would click on and the rifled guns would open fire.

The chain, Gatling thought. An awful lot depended on the first chain. The lead boat would be damaged even if they hit the chain at reduced speed. With the engines full forward, everything above deck would be torn loose and thrown into the river. Everything would go: guns, searchlights, the wheelhouse, the funnel, and the men. It wouldn't win the war, but it would change the odds in the here and now. And that, Gatling thought, was the best they could hope for. If they looked at it realistically, that is.

It got very cold. Here in Saskatchewan the April weather was as unpredictable as it was anywhere else. The *metis* chewed jerked meat and drank cold tea. Dumont told them to get up and get their blood circulating.

The hours of waiting seemed endless; midnight came and went with still no sign of them. A fish jumped in the river and that reminded Dumont of a giant pike he'd caught up north. He started to tell Gatling about it.

"Listen. You hear that?" Gatling cut in.

Dumont heard it, so did the *metis*. A soft throb of engines. The thud of the engines was so muted that it was more a vibration in the air than an actual sound. It got louder as they got closer. The sound remained steady after it reached a certain pitch.

Finally they saw the lead boat, a dark shape on the dark river. It was picking up speed, moving at a faster clip. No lights showed. Gatling looked over at the gun crews. They were ready, so were the riflemen.

Dumont whispered, "You tink dey know where we are?"

"We'll know in a minute," Gatling answered.

It was dark but now the gunboats had definite shapes. Gatling waited for the searchlights to go on. They didn't. The gunboats, keeping to the middle of the river, passed by their position and kept on going. Now the submerged chain was behind them. Suddenly the lead boat went full forward with a fierce thrust of its engines. The smaller boats behind it bobbed in its wake. The searchlight on the lead boat went on. Its powerful beam split the darkness. It moved up from the slope to the fort.

Dumont was counting, trying to figure how long it would take for the lead boat to hit the chain. "One, two, three, four, five, six . . ."

The gunboat hit the chain with tremendous force, and there was an almost-human scream of metal being torn loose. The searchlight went out. The soldiers jammed together on deck screamed and yelled as the chain crushed and mangled their bodies. The searchlights on the smaller boats swung away from the fort and closed in on the big boat up in front. Gatling was able to use the binoculars. The wheelhouse and the funnel had been ripped up and swept off the stern. Men killed or wounded by the chain were sprawled all over the deck. Bodies rolled in the dark river.

Snagged by the chain, the badly damaged gunboat was trying to reverse engines. Water boiled up; the engines roared; they were using all the power they had. The boat broke loose and began to drift. Gatling knew they would find a way to steer the boat from below, but for now, with its wheelhouse gone, the boat was out of control.

Dumont was shaking with excitement. "Dey are getting de chain up. I hear it. Now we have dem." Bells rang furiously on the smaller boats. They reversed engines and were trying to turn. The river was wide enough. They moved slowly, trying to spot the other chain. Somebody up forward saw it and yelled and they reversed engines just in time to avoid being hit. But the damaged boat was drifting toward them. The current was slow and it wasn't moving very fast. A collision, even at that speed, would do some damage.

Gatling opened fire when he knew the men below decks were getting the big gunboat under control. It stopped drifting. The Heavy Maxim and the Hotchkiss went into action; a hundred *metis* rifles spat fire all along the riverbank. The Hotchkiss scored three hits on the big gunboat, now heading for the shore. Bullets spanged off metal plates as the Heavy Maxim raked the deck with bullets. The searchlights on the smaller boats locked in on the *metis* position. Dumont cursed. The rifled cannons and the Gatling started to lay down heavy fire. It got heavier. The first shells exploded behind them, then the gunners corrected and walked the shells in closer. One shell killed five *metis* and wounded seven others. The Hotchkiss gun put the cannon on the second boat out of action after nine tries. Gatling and the *metis* machine-gunner were concentrating on the damaged boat. It was much closer than the others and was heading straight at the riverbank. The soldiers who had come up from below were firing fast from behind any cover they could find. Gatling and the *metis* machine-gunner swept the deck with bullets. The *metis* gunner cursed as his heavy gun suddenly stopped working. "She is jam, she is jam," he cried. "Gatling, you got to fix!"

"Take over." Gatling crawled out from behind his gun. Dumont rolled into position and started firing. Gatling crawled fast. The gunner was slapping the loader. Gatling pulled them apart. "This pig have jam my gun," the gunner shouted. Shells from the third gunboat were thinning out the line of riflemen. The frenzied gunner kept pointing at the jammed Maxim. "His goddamn glove have jam de gun."

A finger from one of the loader's tattered gloves had torn loose and had been pulled into the feed slot with the cartridges. The end of it stuck out through the slot. Gatling pulled hard, but it wouldn't budge. Goddamn it, this was going to take time. Not a lot but some. But there was no time left.

The damaged gunboat ran into shallow water and was held in place by mud. Soldiers were jumping down, firing their rifles while still in the water. Dumont knocked down a line of men. The men behind ran over them. Shells from the third gunboat gave them cover. The smaller boats were running in close. Soon hundreds of men would be on the narrow strip of beach below the bank.

Gatling yelled at Dumont. "We have to pull out! Goddamn you, don't argue about it! We have to pull out!"

Dumont cursed like a madman, but he picked up the light gun and started for the trees at a dead run. The *metis* followed him. The gunners picked up their guns and pulled back. The Hotchkiss was on wheels and it bumped wildly over rough ground. Soldiers were coming up over the riverbank. The searchlights moved in. Concentrated rifle fire came from the riverbank and some of the running *metis* went down. One of the wounded called out after Dumont. Dumont shoved the light gun at Gatling and ran back to get the wounded man.

They were in the trees when Dumont staggered in after them with the wounded man slung over his shoulder. "That man was dead," Gatling told him. Dumont cursed but laid the body down gently. Bullets still came after them, but here the searchlights weren't much use. They had come too far from the river; the soldiers were hanging back. Then a bugle sounded and the soldiers began to pull back to the river.

They got to the fort, crossed the plank bridge over the spiked tranch, then got through the *chevaux-de-frise* and the barbed wire. They took the plank bridge with them before they closed the gap in the *chevaux-de-frise* and went into the fort. Not long after they got inside, one of the gunboats came up the river and shelled the fort for about ten minutes. Then it went back downriver. One man was killed, and three wounded, before the shelling stopped.

The fort was in turmoil; the war that Riel wanted was finally here. Some man told Dumont that Riel wanted to see him as soon as he got back. Dumont ignored him. "I don't got de time to talk 'bout de glorious *metis* nation," he told Gatling. "I got to take look at de wounded. I tink we did not do so well tonight. We lose so many men."

"I don't know," Gatling said. "I'd say we did all right. This wasn't the battle to end the war. That big boat won't be much use to them. It has no heavy guns, no searchlight. It'll have to be towed back to Saskatoon. We destroyed the cannon on the second boat. We killed a lot of men."

"And we lost a lot of men."

"That's how it goes. You can't fight a war without men being killed."

They walked toward the church, which had been turned into a makeshift hospital. The smell of explosives hung in the misty air. Men were still dumping water on fires started by the shells. Other men got in Dumont's way, grabbing at his sleeves, trying to get his attention. They wanted to ask questions about the battle at the river. They wanted to be told they were going to win. They had seen the observation balloon or had heard about it; was it going to fly over Batoche and destroy everything?

Dumont advised them to remain calm, then shunted them off to bother Baptiste. In the church, replacing the benches, camp beds had been set up. The two Irish doctors, Kane and Farrell, attended by the medical orderly, were preparing to amputate the leg of a *metis* who had been hit by shell fragments. The orderly put a makeshift screen around the cot.

Gatling knew that some of the wounded would die. Medical supplies were meager. When the chloroform ran out, they would use whiskey. Men who lived through amputations often died of shock. Dumont moved among the wounded, trying to console those who could hear him. He tried hard, but he wasn't very good at it.

The doctors' smocks were smeared with blood; the floor was slick with blood. A man jumped out of bed, went through the motions of getting dressed, took a few steps, then fell dead. The whole place stank of chloroform and voided bowels.

Outside, Dumont took a deep breath of cold night air. "Gatling, you tink de gunboat will come back tonight."

Gatling said he doubted it. "Not before morning," he said. "Where can we go?"

"Nowhere. Have you got any idea?"

"No good ideas," Gatling said. "Get some sleep. You're carrying too much of a load."

Dumont let loose some French obscenities. "How can I sleep. I'll sleep for a week when dis is over."

"You may sleep longer than that, Gatling thought. But he said nothing.

The smaller gunboats came back at first light. The *metis* were eating breakfast when the first shell exploded against the front wall. The double row of sandbags took the force of the explosion; the wall itself remained intact. A second shell exploded, then a third and a fourth. After that the shells

BORDER WAR

came down like hailstones; they were trying to hit the gate. Gatling knew it wouldn't take them long to do it.

The shelling continued until a wave of men swept out of the woods. All the trees close to the fort had been cut down; the infantrymen had to cross nearly half a mile of open country with no cover of any kind. A second wave of men followed the first. Then a third and fourth wave started out from the trees. A few more shells landed, then the guns were silent.

"Hold your fire," Dumont ordered. "I'll tell you when to fire. You command de heavy guns," he told Gatling.

The attacking regulars hadn't fired a shot; they came forward at a dead run. No one hung back or ran ahead of the others. Gatling ordered the Hotchkiss crew to open fire when the regulars passed the midway mark. The ten-cartridge feed case was already inserted in the loading slot. The huge cartridges dropped down into the gun as the gunner turned the crank handle. The Hotchkiss never jammed. Its mechanism was such that no cartridge followed too closely behind the cartridge in front.

The first shells exploded between the first and second lines of men. Gatling yelled and the gunner corrected the range. The first wave reeled under the rain of shrapnel. Holes appeared in the line as the gunner and the loader found their pace. But the infantry kept coming. Gatling ordered the Maxim crews to start firing. Dumont's riflemen started shooting on his command. The wall of the fort blazed with gun flashes.

Wild screams rang out as the soldiers in the first line fell into the spiked pit. Some of them came to a skidding halt when they saw what it was. The canvas covering had been torn loose. A few of the attackers tried to jump across the ditch; it was too wide. Only one tall soldier got across, and he was cut down while he was still staggering. Now the infantrymen had stopped running and were firing from a kneeling position. They remained calm, aiming before they fired. *Metis* went down under the steady fire. But for the moment the regulars had been stopped. A bugle sounded retreat and they pulled back, pursued by heavy fire. The gunboats opened up again; the shelling went on for more than two hours. But there were no more infantry attacks that day.

The shelling had caused considerable damage. There were gaps in the walls and the gate had been hit several times. Dumont ordered Baptiste to start piling up sandbags behind the gate. "If you run out of bags, pile up anything you can find. Do the same for the walls wherever you can."

Metis were still fighting fires started by the shelling. Except for one or two buildings, Batoche was a wooden town. "Good ting Batoche is so goddamn wet. If dis happen in de dry season, de town would be gone by now. It look like we are in for a long siege."

"Looks like it," Gatling agreed. "I hate to say this. I think more troops will be coming. By river or overland. I think overland. If they had more gunboats they would have sent them. You think I'm right?"

Dumont scowled. "You have been right most of the time. How come you can't be right 'bout something cheerful. But I am force to agree with you. De men dey have here are not enough to take Batoche. Oh, sure, dey could take it if dey wait long enough. Gov'ment will not want to wait. Wait too long and dey will look bad in de newspaper. How long you figure it take dem to get here?"

"A day or two after the next troop train arrives. More than one train may be on its way. More men, more big guns. Maybe real big guns."

"We are lost den, you tink?"

" 'Fraid so." Gatling didn't want to bring up surrender. He felt he had to. "There's nothing dishonorable about it," he said. "Some of the best generals who ever lived surrendered when they had no other choice. It was surrender or let their men be slaughtered. Don't get mad. I don't want to fight you with words or with fists."

Dumont took it calmly. "At dis point I would surrender if I could. But dat is for Louis to decide. I know I have keep on saying dat. But it is de truth."

Gatling said, "You know him better than I do. Is there any chance he'd consider it?"

Dumont shrugged. "Who can tell? I know him and I don't know him. Since he came back from Montana he have change. De consumption, de bad sickness in his lungs. He know he have to die soon. Maybe he want de whole *metis* nation to go 'long with him."

"Son of a bitch! I don't mean Riel."

"I know what you mean," Dumont said. "You are tinking dis terrible war should not have started. But it did. First we tought: 'Hey, we are going to get our freedom. We will make dem treat us like free men.' Den it go on from dere and we want independence. I will tell you the truth because it is getting close to de end. I never believe we could win against de Canadians. But I am a *metis* and could not turn my back on my own people."

"You did your best for them."

"Forget dat. Remember when I told you to get out. You didn't listen to me. So I will say it again: Get out as fast as you can."

"Not yet," Gatling said. "Anyway, the gate can't be opened."

"Shit on you and your jokes," Dumont said. But he wasn't mean about it. "Dis is de last time I will tell you. You don't go soon, maybe you don't go at all."

During daylight hours there was some sniping from the woods. Half a mile was a long way to shoot, but the snipers were using scoped rifles, and one man on the front wall was killed, shot through the head when he stuck it up to take a look. The gunboats came up the river at night, but never stayed long. Usually the shelling lasted no more than 15 minutes. Gatling guessed they were running low on ammunition.

Three days later Dumont discovered that Big Bear had

stolen about half their supplies. The Crees had broken into the storehouse late at night and dropped the stolen supplies over the back wall. This had happened before the gunboats came. Big Bear's men had rearranged the food stocks—sacks of flour and grain, canned goods, and dried meat—so the theft wouldn't be discovered until they were long gone from the fort. On the morning after the theft Big Bear and his Crees rode out.

Dumont and Gatling were in the cabin when Baptiste brought the bad news. Gatling ducked to avoid flying glass when Dumont shattered his whiskey glass on the wall. Dumont got another glass from the cupboard.

"Jesus Christ!" he roared. "If I ever lay my hands on dat pig, I will stuff food down his throat till he explode. Half de supplies have gone. What de hell are we going to do?"

Galting said nothing for a while. Then he said, "Have you talked to Riel?"

Dumont gulped whiskey. "Till I am red in de face. I talk but he don't listen. I argue dat surrender is de only way. We can't let de *metis* be wiped out. Then he look at me and say ver' cold: 'We must fight to de death. If you want to surrender, all you have to do is walk out de gate with a white flag.' You can imagine how I feel. Me dat was with him from de start. Louis don't know what is happening anymore. He don't even know de gate is blocked. Poor Louis, he will find his glorious death pret' soon. Me too. I tink we all die."

Baptiste returned with more bad news: A large force of regulars was assembling in the woods. This force was way back, but it was there. Baptiste said he couldn't be sure, but he guessed about 500 fresh troops had arrived.

Dumont glared at him. "How do you know dis? You say you drop down from de wall and crawl on your belly. You are a crazy man, but all right. Is good information."

This time, Gatling figured, the regulars would be better prepared for an assault on the fort. Out in front of the first wave men would advance with planks to bridge the ditch. They would be covered by heavy fire aimed high. Other men would have bolt-cutters, sheets of canvas to throw over the barbed wire. The attack might be beaten back, but with great loss for the *metis*.

The day dragged by, but there was no attack. Nothing to do but wait. All the waiting was taking its toll in jumpy nerves and frayed tempers. Men quarreled with close friends; there were arguments over food. Food was in everyone's mind; the portions doled out to the men became smaller. The older men were beginning to look very tired. Suicide was almost unknown among the *metis*, but one man shot himself.

The second attack began on the morning of the first day in May. It started with a heavy barrage. Light and heavy cannons had been moved forward during the night; now they filled the air with high explosives. The screaming of the shells rose to a crescendo that drowned out all other sound. On the river the two gunboats were laying down additional fire. As more and more shells hit the fort, men looked as if they wanted to run. A few did run, driven mad by the noise. The men who remained in their positions jeered at them, but everybody wanted to hide in a deep, dark hole.

Casualties were high, and getting higher. So many men were wounded that the hospital couldn't handle them. They lay outside in the mud. Nothing could be done for them. One doctor had been killed, the other badly wounded. The hospital had run out of bandages, chloroform, even whiskey. Some of the wounded had been killed; others would be killed before the shelling stopped.

But it didn't stop. It went on right through the day. The gunners seemed to have limitless amounts of ammunition. It didn't stop even when it got dark and there was heavy rain. The gunners had the range and the shelling continued for another three hours. By now Batoche was a town of shattered buildings, some of them burning. Shell holes pocked the street. And the infantry still hadn't advanced.

The shelling stopped abruptly and Gatling and Dumont

climbed up to the firing platforms. Dead men lay on the platforms, killed by shrapnel or hardwood splinters. The riflemen left on the wall crouched down with their rifles between their legs. Dumont told them to stay where they were. It didn't make much difference what they did.

Dumont looked at the dark woods through a shell hole in the wall. "Dey won't have to send dere troops to attack us," he said. "De big guns will kill us all by dem self."

"They'll attack full force tomorrow," Gatling said. "Everything they have will be thrown at us. The men firing the big guns are artillerymen, but it's an Army picnic. They've come a long way to find a battle. They'll want some glory they can brag about."

Dumont turned to look at the ruined town. "Dis time tomorrow night we'll all be dead."

Not me, Gatling thought.

Chapter TWELVE

Early the next morning a captain with yellow tabs on his collar came in under a flag of truce and demanded their unconditional surrender. He was a youngish man with an unlined red face and a yellow mustache. He wasn't wearing his service revolver. Gatling figured his real reason for coming was to take a look at the fort.

Shouting down from the wall, Dumont told him he would not be allowed inside the fort. Dumont didn't give a reason. Instead, he climbed down a rope and they talked. The red-faced captain repeated his demands: They would lay down their arms and march out of the fort with their hands in the air. He said he spoke with the full authority of the Canadian Government behind him. He said he also spoke on behalf of Her Majesty, Queen of Great Britain and Ireland and Empress of India.

Dumont said no.

The officer stood gaping as Dumont climbed back up the rope and over the wall. Holding himself very stiff, the captain returned to his lines.

"Now we get it good," Dumont said to Gatling.

The barrage started immediately; it looked like the artillerymen were doing their damnedest to blow Batoche off the map. It went for an hour and still the infantry hadn't attacked. The ground under the fort shook every time a shell exploded. Sometimes four or five landed at the same time. Dumont called the *metis* into the poor cover provided by the firing platforms. Fighting to be heard, he told them it was close to the end. If the infantry hadn't attacked by nightfall, any *metis* who wanted to leave should go over the wall and try to make his way to the river. They knew the deep woods, he said, and the Army did not. So there was a chance, a very small chance, that some of them could escape to the north. The food was nearly gone, but an equal amount would be given to every man, and it didn't matter if he stayed or went. They had been brave and loyal and always fine fighting men. He thanked them, and that was all he had to say.

Some of what he said was drowned out by the exploding shells. But the men understood what he was saying, and there were some who squirmed with embarrassment or became angry at the unsaid suggestion that they were cowards. They dispersed and ran for cover as the shells rained down. Bombproofs had been dug but there wasn't enough room for everyone. Fighting broke out at the entrance of one of the shelters. An exploding shell broke it up by killing or wounding ten or more people.

Gatling knew Dumont wasn't speaking for Riel, who remained in the shelter underneath his house. Dumont had given up on Riel. Riel had lost all sense of reality and spent his time reading, or writing speeches, while shells burst overhead. Dumont did send him food, but it remained uneaten.

"I can't help him," Dumont told Gatling. "He live now in his own mind. Last time I saw him he ask me who I am. It make me sad to see him like dat. You know he once want to be a priest, maybe a bishop. People use to say he could be a cardinal if he was not a *metis*. You know dat?"

"I know it."

"When we was young I use to joke with him. Call him Louis de Cardinal. He don't like dat. He is a very holy man. Some of de old people tink he is a saint."

Gatling had nothing to say about that. Louis the Cardinal. Louis the lunatic.

Gatling was thinking he would take Dumont's suggestion and make his way across the line to Alberta. If they didn't catch him, he would board a train bound for Vancouver. There might be delays because of the war. But some passenger trains had to be running. How he would get through the Army lines was something he hadn't figured. A canoe, he thought. If I can get hold of a canoe, maybe I can make it across the river, then head west to Alberta. A canoe or a raft? He didn't have time to make a raft; even if he did build a raft, even a very small one, how would he get it to the river.

Dumont said he would sell his soul for a big glass of whiskey. But he had given the last of his whiskey to the hospital. "I am joke about selling de soul, but I would like a drink. I am nervous. Whiskey would calm me down."

"I wonder why you're nervous," Gatling said.

In spite of the situation, Dumont burst out laughing. "Crazy man," he said. "Always you make de joke? How can you do dat?"

"It's better than whining," Gatling said.

"I feel like whining and crying," Dumont said. "I feel like tearing out my beard."

"You'd look damn peculiar doing that," Gatling said. The shelling began to ease off. The final attack couldn't be far off. He made one last attempt to persuade Dumont not to throw away his life. "They won't kill your people if they don't have to. This is not the Alamo. These soldiers are Canadians. There will be no massacre unless you force it."

Dumont gave Gatling a long look. "You are getting ready to leave? If I may say so, you have picked a bad time to do it. But you have stay for your own reason. How do you tink you will escape?"

"Get to the river, follow it north for a bit, then try to get across. Head west to Alberta."

Dumont shook his head. "No good. Soldiers—militia— will be coming down de north. From Prince Albert. Dey will be watching de river for *metis* trying to escape. No more rebellion if dey round up all de *metis*. Dey catch you quick, Gatling."

"What do you have in mind?"

"Here is a plan," Dumont said. "Not so good, all dere is. When de attack come, dis last attack, get over de wall. De town will be burning from de shells. Plenty smoke everywhere. I pray God give you fog or rain. But you will have plenty smoke. Do not run to de river. Crawl to it. Find a hiding place under de bank. Not far upstream dere are reeds. Get in dere and wait. Take your pistol, all you take, hear me. Long guns do you no good. You have to leave de gun in de case."

Dumont knew how much Gatling depended on the modified light machine gun. "I'll have to think about that," Gatling said.

Dumont shrugged. "Do what you like, Gatling. I am telling you what I would do. Now. Dere are some canoes here in Batoche. Dey are in a shed to protect dem from snow and rain. You have seen dem? Good. Den I don't have to show you. We have to give de *metis* a chance to use dem. Dey won't. If nobody want dem, then you smash up all but one canoe. Pile broken canoe on top of de good one. Soldiers won't bother with broken canoes. If dey don't catch fire, then you have good canoe when you come back."

Gatling let Dumont talk.

"Could be a long wait for you. Nothing you can do. Now listen to dis part. Dey will start de infantry attack and we will give up. Sound crazy. Never mind. I have decide. Fight to de death? But we have to show de world dat *metis* fight till dey have nothing left to fight with. Soldiers will tell us to march out, hands up. Okay. You go over de back wall when dat is going on. I don't tink dey will burn de rest of de town. Dey do what dey like. If town is burning, dey won't try to put out de fire. No way dey can. Dey will not try."

Gatling just nodded. It wasn't a bad plan. It had a lot of *ifs* in it, but what desperate plan did not.

Dumont said. "After we march out, dey will post a guard over de town. Dey will search de town, look in de underground shelters. But you will be at de river by dat time. Dey don't find anybody in de town 'cept dead men. Who can say how big a guard dey will leave? No so many men, I tink. Now come de hard part. In de night you have to come back, get out de canoe is not damage, and get it to the river."

"I may have to wait more than one night," Gatling said.

"You may have to wait plenty of night if dey leave big party here. Not likely. But dey will leave some guard. Maybe you should wait till all guard leave. Is a risk what you have to do. Canoe is light but big. You must decide. You have canoe, you can cross de river. One thing you got to remember. Get away before de militia arrive. Dey will burn de town for sure."

The shelling had stopped. Dumont unslung his Mauser. "Dey are coming, so I will say goodbye now. I am grateful for all you have done."

They shook hands and Dumont left to take up his position on the wall. Gatling watched him as he climbed up the ladder. The *metis* riflemen followed him, though some hung back, confused and frightened, not knowing what to do. Gatling thought: It's one thing to be ready to die, but it's hard to get through it. Far out from the fort the regulars were yelling. They were coming in for a frontal assault. They expected resistance, but nothing could stop them and they knew it.

The shed where the canoes were hadn't been hit by shell fire. Long, light canoes were piled high. He picked up a chunk of wood and started to smash in the fragile sides. Now all but one were destroyed. He piled the wreckage on top of the sound canoe and started for the back wall. There was no one there; Dumont had ordered everyone forward. Gatling was crouching down behind a row of barrels when the infantry opened fire. On the wall the *metis* began to shoot back. The Maxim guns opened up.

Gatling looked at the leather case that lay beside him. Dumont had advised him not to take the light gun. But he would. Maybe it would be the death of him, yet he hated to leave it behind. Far from being superstitious, he didn't believe in good or bad luck. He just didn't want to abandon a weapon that had proved so reliable. The leather case had seen some hard use; so had the sample cases carried by most traveling salesmen; and when the bipod was folded back and the ammunition box removed, it was no longer or larger than many cases used for bulky items.

He went up to the firing platform, and from there he could see the river. On all sides of the fort the land had been cleared. Not a bush or rock remained above ground. Behind him, at the other end of the fort, the firing eased off, then stopped. A bugle sounded and there was shouting. They would be clearing the gate in a few minutes.

He dropped the gun case into a drift of dirty snow that still clung to the base of the wall. Then he dropped down beside it and waited. He couldn't see the gunboats, but they'd be moving in close to the riverbank. There was a screeching noise as the wrecked gate was dragged open. Crawling, dragging the gun case with one hand, he started for the river. By now there was a lot of shouting inside the fort, but he didn't look back. No point. If they spotted him from the wall, there was no way they could miss, well-trained regulars with rifles.

Now he was about halfway to the river. Bracing himself for the shock of bullets, he kept going until he reached the bank and slid down into the reeds. Only then did he look back. There was no wind and a pall of smoke hung over the fort. A single rifle cracked, but whether the shot was fired by a *metis* or a soldier, he had no way of knowing. Faces appeared over the top of the wall, and a few minutes later a squad of soldiers came around from the front of the fort. They looked around and went away.

One of the soldiers on the wall was scanning the river and the woods with binoculars. Gatling burrowed down in the reeds and tried to stay warm. If the wind blew up or it started to rain he would be a lot colder than he was. It might even snow. He had stuffed dried meat in his coat pocket but he wasn't hungry yet. One thing he wouldn't run short of was water. He didn't look forward to drinking freezing river water, but he'd be glad to drink it after he ate some of the dried, heavily salted deer meat.

Hours later, when it was getting dark, the gunboats pulled out; the sound of their engines was lost in the great stillness of the river and the woods. Smoke still hung over the fort. It got colder and it looked like rain. The rain started and it came down heavy, and he watched it falling in the dark river. He chewed on dried meat and drank water from scooped hands. He was saving his canteen water for later.

It was dark but still too early to try anything; he might not be able to get the canoe tonight or even tomorrow. But he would take a look and then decide. He knew he could wait as long as he had to if the temperature didn't drop back to freezing. If that happened he would have to make his move. He'd often heard it said that freezing to death was painless, but it wasn't a theory he wanted to test by doing it himself. Better a bullet than to end up a frozen corpse.

There was no sign that the rain would stop anytime soon. But it wouldn't freeze as long as it rained. By now he was soaked clear through; his boots were full of water. It was a waste of time to take them off and empty them out, because they'd just fill up again.

He crawled up to take a look at the fort. The fires had

gone out and the fort was dark, yet he knew the soldiers left to guard it would have a fire going somewhere, probably in one of the buildings that hadn't been damaged by shell fire. They were regulars, and would guard the town as ordered, but for now they would stay out of the rain. They would make their rounds and then go back to steam themselves dry at the fire.

Gatling decided to try for the canoe before the rain stopped, and though he hated the rain, it was the only thing he had in his favor. He left the gun case where it was, and when he was up and over the riverbank he ran toward the deep shadow of the wall. Inside the fort there wasn't a sound. He waited and listened but there was nothing.

One swing dropped the looped rope over one of the pointed logs that made up the wall. He was over the wall and climbing down the ladder from the firing platform when he heard them coming. He ran for cover behind the row of barrels and lay flat on the mud. There were two of them and one was saying, "What I wouldn't give for a hot meal and a warm bed! How long d'ye think they'll keep us here?"

"As long as they bloody well please," the other soldier said bitterly. "Ours not to reason why, or hadn't you heard?"

Gatling had the Colt in his hand, and he would kill them if he had to. Then he would run for the woods and head north, not that dodging and hiding would do him any good. But it didn't come to killing, not yet anyway, and after a while the two soldiers moved on. He gave them a few minutes before he headed for the shed where the canoe was.

The rain drumming on the galvanized-iron roof covered the noise he made dragging the wrecked canoes away from the sound one. He balanced the canoe on his head, gripped the sides with both hands, and got it as far as the ladder. He went up backwards, dragging the canoe after him. If they came along now they'd have him dead to rights, but nothing happened. He roped the canoe securely and lowered it to the ground. Nobody challenged him as he carried the canoe to the river.

The current was moving the broken-up ice; he had to paddle and ward off slabs of ice with jagged edges at the same time. Even a short slash along the fragile sides of the canoe would send it to the bottom, and he knew he wouldn't survive for more than three or four minutes in the freezing water. But he got across, and after he picked up the gun case he kicked a hole in the canoe and pushed it out into deep water. It filled up and sank.

He picked up the road to North Battleford where it came down from the north. Up ahead there was a low, crumbling cliff, and when he got to it, he climbed a brushy slope looking for a place to spend the night. Somehow he had to get his clothes and boots dry. A cold, pale moon gave some light as he made his way along the base of the cliff. He found a deep hole that wasn't a natural cave but had been made by the collapse of the rock face. Inside it was dry, and brush and twigs had been blown in by the wind.

He got a small fire going with a match from his watertight match case. Even though the case was guaranteed to be waterproof, some of the matchheads were soft and he laid them on a flat stone to dry out. He piled on more twigs and then went out to root up brush to keep the fire going. He broke off pieces of brush and put them on the fire before he went back down to the road and looked up at his hiding place. The rockfall all but covered the entrance to the cave. He saw nothing.

A fissure that went up to the top of the cliff carried off the smoke. The cave was dry and soon it was warm. He stripped off and hung his clothes from small branches that would be used as firewood. He would have to buy or steal better-looking clothes before he boarded the train. The clothes he had were caked with mud and ripped in several places. Even if he tried to pass as a dirt-poor homesteader, he'd still look like a hobo. And what would a hobo be doing with a salesman's sample case?

But how he looked was something to think about tomorrow. For now, he was warm and dry; as far as he knew, there was nobody dogging him. He chewed jerked meat and drank from the canteen. He wanted to sleep but that was too risky. It would be a hell of a thing to be chased bare-assed through the woods.

Finally his clothes were dry enough to put on, and he stretched out and slept. By morning the rain had stopped and the fire was out. He had to face a hard wind when he went down to the road, but the country was thawing out, and it wasn't too bad. Not much farming was done between the river and North Battleford, Dumont had told him, and the few farms in that part of the country had been abandoned. Now that the war was over these farm families would be coming back, but not just yet, he figured; it was the militia he had to watch out for.

There was no sign of any recent traffic, and he walked all day without seeing anybody. That night he slept for a few hours, without a fire, without shelter. He ate the last of the salty meat before he started out hours before first light. That day and the day after were the same; he saw no one.

Finally he reached the bend in the road, where it went northwest to North Battleford. He followed a smaller road going south, and it was narrow, not much more than a track, but it was safer than the road that went to the fort. By this time, the fort would be reoccupied by the military, regulars or militia, and the Mounted Police would be back. If any of the *metis* garrison had escaped, they would be combing the woods, trying to find them, and from here on he could expect to be shot at.

That night, huddled behind a rock, he heard shooting far off in the woods. After it stopped, he got a few hours' sleep. Later he saw hoofprints that came out of the woods and went on ahead of him before going back into the trees. What he had to watch out for was a party of men in a fixed position, regulars or militiamen stopping anyone who came along. With North Battleford in their minds, the militia might not bother with questions. Late on the following day he nearly walked into such a trap, but they had a small fire going and he was able to circle their position without being seen.

The road went through a long stretch of sand hills that would be like a desert in summer. There was no water here and he drank sparingly from the canteen. No signposts told him where he was going, but he figured he was in Alberta. Dumont had told him that Medicine Hat would be the best place to board the train. It was a fairly big town and he was less likely to be noticed at the depot.

Now he was in settled country and could travel only at night. His belly rumbled with hunger, but it was too dangerous to try to buy or beg food at a farmhouse, and though the war hadn't touched Alberta, people there would be jittery and suspicious. He had come too far to be killed by a nervous farmer armed with a shotgun.

But it came close to that, though the man who tried to kill him was no sodbuster. It happened just after he came to a signpost that pointed to Medicine Hat. Ten more miles to go. He still hadn't done a damn thing about his clothes. Maybe he could get a shave and new clothes before he boarded the train. There would be food on the train; the thought of ham and eggs and hot coffee made him walk faster.

He could see the smoke of the town, no more than three or four miles in the distance, when he heard a horse galloping far behind him. He was off the road, crouched down in the brush, and the rider was getting closer. The man on the horse had a rifle in his hand; a bottle stuck out of his pocket. Gatling thought he was going to ride on, but he turned the horse off the road and came straight in at full tilt. Gatling got off one shot with the Colt before the frightened horse rode over him, kicking and plunging. A steel-shod hoof knocked the gun from Gatling's hand and he got a hard kick in the thigh. He was scrambling for the Colt and was close to getting it when the rider fired one shot from his Winchester carbine and levered another round into the chamber.

"Get up," the rider ordered.

Gatling got up and turned to face him. The man holding the carbine was in his forties, carefully shaved, and had crazy eyes. He was very drunk, but the short gun in his hand was steady enough. Gatling started to say something, but the rider roared at him to be silent.

"Silent, I say," the man roared, frightening the horse even more. Spittle flew from the man's mouth and some of it remained on his chin. "You know what I'm going to do to you, you filthy vagrant scum. Or are you a *metis*? We've been warned. That's what you are, a crawling, treacherous half-breed mongrel. Sneaking away from your rotten, so-called rebellion. When I think of the good men you've killed! But you'll kill no more, you disloyal rubbish. This is where you die."

"The rebellion is over," Gatling said. "Nothing to do with me. I'm just a bum." The man with the carbine wasn't just drunk, he was out of his mind. His clothes were good, black wool suit, short wool topcoat. Certainly no ordinary farmer.

"That doesn't concern me," the man said. "You are on my land, a dangerous trespasser, and that gives me the right to shoot you. This is my land and I do what I like. Nobody crosses me and gets away with it. My neighbors don't like me because I drink too much. Nobody likes me, matter of fact, and I glory in it. But even my sour-faced Presbyterian neighbors can't object if I shoot down a lice-ridden *metis*, now can they?"

The man was insane but Gatling had to give it a try. "I'm not a *metis*. Do I sound like a *metis*? Look, mister, I'm sorry for coming on your land. I'm just a 'bo. Let me go and you'll never see me again."

"I don't care what you are, I have the right to kill you. What's in that case? Open it."

Gatling pretended to fumble with the metal snaps. "Get a move on, you foul bastard." The man rode in closer as Gatling opened the case. "Get back," the man said.

He was still staring at the light machine gun when Gatling

swept off his hat and slapped the horse across the muzzle. The horse reared up and plunged away and began to run. Gatling was grabbing the Colt when the man was flung from the saddle, hit the ground, and lay still.

Gatling looked around and saw nothing but desolate farmland under a gloomy sky. If the shots had been heard, nobody was coming to see who was shooting at what. The man was dead, his neck broken by the fall.

Gatling stripped the body and dressed himself in the dead man's clothes. He left the dead man's personal belongings beside the body. The clothes weren't a bad fit; they would pass. Later, when the neighbors or the police found the body, most likely they would put it down as a drunken accident. The fact that he was naked might not even puzzle them. He had been a wild, crazy drunk who did crazy things.

Gatling picked up the gun case and walked the rest of the way to Medicine Hat.

He got back to New York.

Chapter THIRTEEN

"They hanged Riel this morning," Colonel Pritchett said. "O'Brien just got it on the wire. His third appeal was turned down, so he's dead. The insanity plea didn't work after all. A huge crowd gathered outside the prison while it was still dark. I never thought he was crazy. They were determined to hang him. They would have hanged him if he'd been as crazy as a loon."

Gatling was slouched in a leather chair across the desk from the colonel. He didn't give a damn about Riel, though the man obviously wasn't right in the head. He had brought a firestorm down on the *metis*; they wouldn't recover from it for years.

"What about Gabriel Dumont?" Gatling had written to the big *metis*; there had been no replies. Dumont had been tried and convicted of treason and many other charges. He was being held in the same prison in Regina where Riel was executed.

"Well, they gave him life," the colonel said. "But you know that. It's been in the papers. There is a movement to have his sentence reduced. Petitions, appeals to the Prime Minister, that sort of thing. The Government up there wants to put this unpleasantness behind it. French Canada—Quebec—is all stirred up. Some believe there is hope of a pardon after Dumont has served part of his sentence. By the way, O'Brien tells me the fifty thousand dollars you sent to Dumont's lawyers was returned this morning. It seems the Government put pressure on them. O'Brien tried to hire better lawyers, but was informed that the lawyers Dumont has now must remain."

Gatling said, "It's strange to think of Dumont having to rely on lawyers."

The colonel raised his bushy eyebrows. "Did he want to act as his own lawyer? I'm sure he doesn't know a thing about the law. Of course it would have been the same no matter who argued the case."

Gatling said, "Dumont didn't want to do anything. He told them to hang him and get it over with. But the Government insisted that he have lawyers. Dumont just sat there and didn't say a word all through the trial."

"That's right," the colonel said. "His lawyers argued that he was a simple not-too-bright poor fellow who'd been led down the garden path by the sinister Riel. He tried to smash up the court when he heard that. The judge ordered him gagged and bound. I take it you feel great sympathy for the fellow."

Gatling wanted to pick up the desk and throw it at the colonel. "His name is Gabriel Dumont, not 'fellow.' I liked him all right. He had a terrible temper and could be a pain in the ass, but he was all right. You could trust him to do what he said."

"Most commendable. He must have been a fine man in his way."

"You could say that, Colonel. But what's the use of talking about it. I doubt if he'll ever see the North Woods again."

The colonel had Gatling's report on his desk. "I've skimmed through this," he said. "Tonight I'll give it my undivided attention. Meanwhile, can you fill me in on a few details? Your report on the Mauser seems to be most favorable. But you still have reservations about the Officer's Model thirty-eight. You say it doesn't have enough stopping power."

"It doesn't. Sure it can kill a man. Any gun can kill a man. But I don't feel it's right for combat. Suppose an Apache that's been eating crazy mushrooms comes screaming at you. All he wants to do is kill you. He doesn't give a damn about his own life. He doesn't even think about it. He's wild, he's crazy, and he's bearing down on you like an express train. I don't think the thirty-eight is going to stop him. You may be dead before he is."

"Well, I'll certainly mention it to Mr. Maxim." The colonel wrote a few lines in a notebook. He laughed. "What about the Horseshoe Pistol? Odd-looking thing, isn't it."

"It saved my life," Gatling said. He told the colonel about the fight on the prairie. He was scouting the country far south of Batoche and was caught in a militia ambush. "My horse was killed and fell on my rifle. My forty-five was empty. I killed a whole bunch of them with the odd-looking pistol, as you call it."

The colonel started fooling with his pipe; with him, it was some sort of ceremony. "Amazing. Absolutely amazing," he said. "But it's still a peculiar-looking weapon. You think it has any commercial value?"

"I doubt it. It's the look of the gun that's against it. People like their weapons to have clean lines. Maybe you could manufacture it in limited quantities."

The colonel got his curved pipe going and he sighed with satisfaction. "Oh, well, that decision is up to Mr. Maxim. What about the Balloon Gun?"

"I shot down one balloon. One balloon was all there was. It was close enough during the last days of the siege. I guess they knew we were just about out of ammunition. They sent it up in darkness. It was there in the morning. I dropped over the wall, crawled closer, and shot it down. I had to dodge like hell to get back.''

"Good show," the colonel said. He said it all the time. He would have said it at a dogfight. He would have said it when Wellington defeated Bonaparte at Waterloo.

"It must have been a peculiar little war," the colonel remarked. "Good Lord! It must have been cold there. I hate cold. I spent so many years in India. From what I've read, Saskatchewan must be a miserable place. Hardly worth fighting about, what?"

"The *metis* wouldn't agree with you, Colonel. A lot of them died for it. Nobody knows what'll happen to them now. They're holding them in camps. They'll probably get some bad land and be watched all the time. The Government doesn't want a new messiah to arise. That won't be Dumont. If he gets out he'll disappear. He never wanted the war, but once it started, he did his best. You think O'Brien can get money to him some other way?"

The colonel didn't like the question. "If I were you I'd stay out of it. It's over, finished, already in the past. You're lucky you aren't in prison with Dumont. The Fenians were deported, but you wouldn't be treated so lightly. I doubt if there would be any pardon for you. Washington has made a most sincere apology. From now on any American renegade who tries to make political trouble in Canada will be extradited and severely punished. That means you, my lad. Think of cold, damp cells. Think of beans three times a day."

Gatling pushed his chair back so hard it fell over. "You have a new assignment, you can get me at the hotel. If there's any problem you can find me in Denver."

"Wait a moment," the colonel said. "I have some interesting news that quite slipped my mind. By now the Canadian Government will have linked us to the rebellion. I suppose that was inevitable. What astonishes me is the fact that the Canadians are prepared to forgive and forget."

Gatling had his hand on the doorknob. "Why is that?"

"They are impressed by what our Maxims and Hotchkiss guns did to their troops. Cold-blooded bastards, but who gives a damn. Hang onto your hat, old fellow. They have just placed an order for a very large shipment of weapons. What do you think of that?"

"I think this time you should deliver them yourself." Gatling opened the door and slammed it behind him.

The World's Greatest Western Writer

ZANE GREY

Classic tales of action and adventure
set in the Old West
and penned with blistering authority
by America's Master Story Teller

THE BUFFALO HUNTER. Rugged, dangerous men and the beasts they hunted to the point of extinction.

_____2599-X $2.75 US/$3.75 CAN

SPIRIT OF THE BORDER. The settlers were doomed unless a few grizzled veterans of the Indian Wars, scalphunters as mean and vicious as the renegades, could stop them.

_____2564-7 $2.75 US/$3.75 CAN

THE RUSTLERS OF PECOS COUNTY. Although outnumbered a thousand to one, the Texas Rangers were the last chance the settlers had. It had to be enough.

_____2498-5 $2.75 US/$3.50 CAN

THE LAST RANGER. The classic frontier tale of a brutal Indian fighter and a shrewd beauty who struggled to make a heaven of the hell on earth they pioneered.

_____2447-0 $2.95 US/$3.75 CAN

THE LAST TRAIL. White renegades stir up the hostile Indian tribes surrounding the little settlement of Fort Henry.

_____2636-8 $2.95 US/$3.95 CAN

LEISURE BOOKS
ATTN: Customer Service Dept.
276 5th Avenue, New York, NY 10001

Please send me the book(s) checked above. I have enclosed $_____
Add $1.25 for shipping and handling for the first book: $ .30 for each book thereafter. No cash, stamps, or C.O.D.s. All orders shipped within 6 weeks. Canadian orders please add $1.00 extra postage.

Name _____
Address _____
City_____State_____Zip_____

Canadian orders must be paid in U.S. dollars payable through a New York banking facility. ☐ Please send a free catalogue.